GW00806387

Dead Dream Girl

Dead Dream Girl

Richard Haley

ROBERT HALE · LONDON

ISBN 978-0-7090-8310-8

Robert Hale Limited
Clerkenwell House
Clerkenwell Green
London EC1R 0HT

For Grace, Georgina and Sam

Typeset in 11/15½pt Palatino
Printed and bound in Great Britain by
Biddles Limited, King's Lynn

O N E

The body was winched out of the water very slowly on a flat board. Skilled divers had manoeuvred it on to the board with great care, after first untying the cords that had attached the body to a bag of stones. The frogmen had been anxious to ensure that no further damage was accidentally caused to the body than had happened at the time it was thrown in. Autopsy examinations in the search for clues to a possible identity of the killer would be complicated enough as it was.

The body still wore a summer dress. It was torn and mud-stained, but a woman among the small group looking on was able to detect that it hadn't been cheap. It was drop-waisted and had elegant button work down the bodice and a finely etched floral pattern.

The body's face was bloated and had the sort of pitting and scarring that had probably been inflicted by predatory pond life. It was just possible, in the early autumn sunlight, to tell that the hair was honey coloured. The SOC team, standing grim faced on the reservoir bank, needed none of these sparse details to tell them whose body it was. It could only be that of Donna Jackson, a woman their CID colleagues had been searching for for weeks. A boy, a keen underwater swimmer, had found it. Children were forbidden to swim in the reservoir, but they did anyway. If it hadn't been for the boy, one of the onlookers muttered sourly, the poor kid's body would have been down there for good.

Frank Crane drove on to Willow Tree Park on an evening in June. It was an attractive name for what was a council estate, always known by locals as the Willows. It was on the edge of Bradford and near the green belt, but that hadn't stopped it going to the dogs exactly like the inner city ones. It had just taken longer, that was all. There were still pockets of respectability, but too many problem families had sidled their way in, who used the gardens as storage dumps for old tyres and rusting car parts, and kept vicious-looking dogs on chains. Their children lived a life of their own, mainly in packs of ten on street corners.

Garden Drive was in the middle of the estate and looked to be one of the better bits. The Jacksons lived at number 27. Crane had been told they were decent, hardworking people, and this seemed to be confirmed by a neatly clipped hedge, a newly mown lawn and flowered borders. The house was a small boxy semi, like all the others, and Crane could only park his car with difficulty about twenty yards away on the crowded roadside.

He walked up a narrow, flagged pathway and pressed the bell of a cream-painted door. He didn't hear a ring tone and it went unanswered. He knocked. The door was then slowly drawn open, as if not much used. He guessed that the Jacksons' normal visitors knew to use the side door.

'Mrs Jackson? I'm Frank Crane.'

'Oh ... hello,' she said nervously. 'Come in, please.'

She was spare and smallish and had dark brown hair

which had an inch-wide strand of grey running from the right temple. Hollow cheeks emphasized a knobbly bone structure and her hazel eyes were haunted looking above a long nose. She wore a faded zip-front navy shirt and well-worn, stone-coloured cords.

She turned and led him along a short narrow hallway and into the back room. It looked like it doubled as living and dining room. A man sat at a small drop-leaf table in front of the window and a young woman sat in an armchair watching *Coronation Street*. She reluctantly switched it off with a remote. 'It's all right,' she said, to no one in particular. 'I'm taping it anyway.'

'This is Mr Crane, Malc,' Mrs Jackson said, still nervous.

'Pleased to meet you, Mr Crane,' he said, getting up and holding out a hand. He was smallish but stocky, in trousers and T-shirt, with heavy glasses that slightly enlarged pale blue eyes, blunt, reddish features and greying dark hair. His hand shook slightly. He seemed as uneasy as his wife.

'And this is Patsy,' Mrs Jackson went on. Patsy gave him an indifferent smile, her eyes not quite meeting his.

'I'm sorry you've had to come in the evening,' Jackson said, 'but with us all working ... Connie could have had some time off, but we all wanted to be here, know what I mean?'

'Don't worry, Mr Jackson. I do a good deal of my work in the evening.'

'Call me Malc. And this is Connie.'

'And I'm Frank.'

'Will you take a drink, Frank? Beer? Whisky?'

Crane never normally drank while working, but he felt drinks would help them to relax for what could be a demanding interview. 'A beer would be fine.'

'I'll see to it, Dad.' Patsy got up. 'How about you, Mam?'

Connie shrugged indifferently. 'I'll have a small Bristol Cream, pet, if there's any left.'

Patsy went through to the kitchen and the three of them stood in silence. Crane was used to this awkward moment, when people were steeling themselves to talk about emotional or embarrassing situations. He had ways of putting them at their ease, but Connie suddenly said, 'Show him the papers, Malc.'

'They're here, Frank. I got them ready.'

The papers were insurance statements. Crane caught the figure £10,000 Sum Assured, and the words 'plus accumulated bonus to date'. Puzzled, he glanced from the papers to Malc's uneasy, enlarged eyes. 'It's due in a week or two, Frank, do you see?' he said anxiously. 'So we can pay you, no problem, if you don't mind hanging on till they pay us.'

'We don't care how much it costs,' Connie said flatly. 'We wanted it for a down payment on a house of our own, right away from the Willows, but nothing comes before putting that swine behind bars where he belongs.'

'That's right, Frank,' Malc said, his voice breaking slightly. 'We couldn't live with ourselves if we didn't do everything possible.'

Crane looked at their anxious faces. He'd thought long and hard about coming here. Terry Jones had already told him they'd have to break into their nest egg to pay his fees. But he'd also said they were determined to have a private man and if Crane didn't take the case they might land themselves with someone who'd take the money and walk through it. In the end he knew it was the challenge that had drawn him. His challenge, their tragedy, that was the sad bit.

'I don't need any proof you have the money. I know respectable people when I see them. What I need to tell you is that I can only accept the work when I've talked it over carefully with you. I need to decide if I can be of genuine help. If I do act for you I'll explain exactly how much it will cost. And ... well ... I'd also like to say how deeply sorry I am about your daughter.'

Neither spoke, their faces impassive, their eyes unfocused, but a sense of powerful emotion seemed to thicken the air like humidity. It was a relief when Patsy came in with the drinks on a battered tin tray. She offered it to Crane with the same non-connecting smile as before. She was tall, with her mother's brown hair, which she'd sprayed into a tousled style that did nothing for her. She had regular but completely plain features, apart from eyes that were a shade of lavender. She was aggressively made up as if trying to force prettiness on to her modest looks. She wore a wrinkled slash-neck cotton sweater in green and white stripes and grubby white bell-bottom trousers.

'Sit down, Frank,' Connie said finally, on a near-strangled note. A small three piece had been crammed into the little room, which also had a sideboard and a stereo, as well as the television. The wall pictures were of the type that came from chain stores. Crane sat in one of the armchairs, Malc in the other, the women on the sofa. They seemed as packed together as people sitting in the corner of a crowded pub.

'You will take it, Frank, won't you?' Connie spoke in a low urgent voice. 'Mr Benson wouldn't have mentioned your name if he'd not thought you could help.'

'Worked the clock round, DS Benson,' Malc said huskily. 'Couldn't have done no more. None of them lads could.'

Crane nodded, remembering the time when Benson had been grey with fatigue, when there'd been a task force, an incident room, endless overtime. He said, 'I'm going to have to bring back painful memories. I know there's been a question mark hanging over Donna's boyfriend – Bobby Mahon, wasn't it?'

'He *did* it, Frank,' Malc broke out. 'No question. Even DS Benson said they weren't looking for no one else in the end. I tell you, I'd have seen to the sod myself, except it'd only have brought more upset to Mam here and Patsy.'

'Dad …' Patsy put a hand on his trembling arm.

'It's the truth, Frank,' Connie almost whispered, her eyes moist in declining sunlight. 'She … she came home with bruises more than once, a black eye, a swollen face. We had to keep her out of Malc's way till we got her looking right again, he'd have gone round there and smashed him.'

'Too right,' he muttered. 'Too bloody right.'

'He said she was two-timing him, that Mahon,' Connie went on. 'But she wasn't. She was a bonny girl. She couldn't help it if men couldn't take their eyes off her.'

Crane caught Patsy's glance. Her face was expressionless. She said, 'Anyway, he was two-timing *her*. Seemed to think he could do as he chose.'

Crane said, 'How did he take it … when Donna was found?'

'Cracked on to be heartbroken,' Malc said bitterly. 'Round here every verse end when they had to let him go. Swearing it wasn't him, over and over again. He could even turn the waterworks on. Crying. Always round here crying.'

'I think it was genuine, Dad,' Patsy said. 'I'm sure he

was upset, even if he did do it. That was Bobby's trouble, it was just the same when he landed her one, pleading and sobbing for her to take him back.'

Crane glanced at her. It was a good point. He knew from experience that bad hats often did show remorse about a killing while stubbornly denying it was down to them. It didn't mean the remorse was any less valid. He took out his notebook. 'What was Donna's job?'

'She worked at Leaf and Petal.'

'Garden centre, off Back Lane?'

'That's the one,' Malc said heavily. 'Helped in and among. Told folk where things were, worked a checkout, gave a hand in the café.'

'She was doing grand,' Connie said, wiping an eye with a knuckle. 'She was doing grand. It's seasonal for most of the young ones, what with the winter months being so quiet, but Mr Hellewell said he'd keep her on that last winter, teach her about the plants and the young trees. Told her she had a really good future.'

Patsy's face was expressionless again.

'Nice bloke, Joe Hellewell,' Malc said. 'Really took Donna under his wing.'

'She did some modelling work as well,' Connie added.

'That was Clive,' Malc told him. 'Just calls himself Clive. Has that photography shop on Shilling Street.'

'He was positive he could make a name for her,' Connie said, with the same sad pride as before. 'He was sending pictures of her to the people who do the mail-order catalogues. That would be a start, he told her, there was no telling where she'd end up.'

Crane didn't need to check Patsy's expression this time. He knew it would be stonier than ever.

'So … she worked at Leaf and Petal during the day and did her modelling in her spare time … evenings, days off?'

They nodded. 'She were never in,' Malc said, trying to mask his pain with an indulgent smile. 'Never in. Off to her work, off to her modelling, off clubbing. I used to say, "The only time you spend an evening with your mum and dad, young lady, is when you're poorly."'

'And she hardly ever *was* poorly,' Patsy added. 'Can't remember the last time she had a cold.'

'Should have caught pneumonia,' Malc said, forcing a chuckle, 'some of the skimpy things she'd go off in, middle of winter.'

'How long had she known Bobby Mahon?'

'He'd always been around. Lives in the next road. She got to know him properly at the Goose and Guinea. We never liked her going, not with the class of riff-raff goes in there these days, but what can you do?'

'Tanglewood,' Crane said. 'Did she ever go along by the reservoir before she …?'

'They'd go Sunday afternoons now and then, to walk the Mahons' dog. It's popular with folk who keep a dog.'

'Is it likely she'd go there after dark? Of her own free will?'

Malc sighed, clearly struggling for self-control. 'Mahon … he could talk her into things.'

'She'd not have gone, left to herself,' Connie said harshly. 'Apart from anything else, you don't know *who* goes in there after dark.'

'Oh, I don't know, Mam,' Patsy said evenly. 'She could be more than a bit wild, you know she could.'

'She wasn't wild, Patsy. She was just high-spirited, liked

a laugh, that's all. I'm positive she'd not have wanted to go in that spooky place after dark.'

'Get me another drink, Patsy love,' Malc said, his voice wavering. 'I'm sorry, Frank, it's always the same when we start talking about our precious little Donna.'

Patsy glanced at Crane's glass. Seeing it was still half-full she went off without a word. Crane said, 'I really am very sorry to have to put you through it all again.'

'You need to know the details,' Connie said, tears now trickling steadily down her hollow cheeks. 'She was so pretty, Frank, so full of life. How *anyone* could …'

Crane worked hard to detach himself from the unhappiness of some of the people he dealt with, but didn't always succeed when the emotion was this raw. 'I … think I have everything I need to be going on with,' he said. 'I just needed an outline of her life and work.'

Patsy put Malc's refilled glass into his trembling hand. She said, 'There was a lot in the *Standard* about it.'

'Yes, I remember the reports.'

'The bloke who wrote them, they call him Geoff Anderson. He spent an awful lot of time on it. Came here once or twice to talk to Mam and Dad. Keen as mustard to see someone nailed. Might be worth your while having a word with him. Nice bloke.'

'I'll do that.'

'Lived and breathed it, Frank, same as DS Benson. Spent a long time with Mam and me, just going over her life so he could write it all up. There were times he could hardly get a word out himself, what with being that upset over Mam and me in tears, but Patsy managed to tell him what he needed to know.'

Crane stood up. 'Well, I'll do the best I can.'

'You'll work for us?'

'I have to remind you, Malc, that a team of highly skilled policemen have spent a lot of time on Donna's death. All I can really do is go over the ground again and see if there's anything they might just have missed.'

'You might be able to find enough for us to bring a private prosecution. Mr Benson explained that to us as well.'

'You'd go that far?'

'As far as it takes.'

'All right, Malc. Now I must explain my charges.'

He gave them detailed figures, and an estimate of expenses. Even middle-class people usually winced at the bottom line, but the Jacksons took it without reaction. 'Whatever it costs, Frank,' Malc said, dabbing at his eyes with a handkerchief. 'As long as you don't mind hanging on till the Pru poppies up. We'll spend it all, if need be.'

'We couldn't live with ourselves if we didn't feel we'd done everything we could,' Connie said quietly. 'If you can't get anywhere either we'll call it a day.'

Patsy, who'd been briefly absent, came back into the small room wearing a lightweight indigo parka. 'I'll see you out,' she said. 'Then I'll go on to Debbie's, Mam.'

Crane said his goodbyes and walked with her along the short path. 'Can I give you a lift?'

'No, she just lives on the end. Thanks all the same.'

It was in Crane's direction so they walked together. 'It's been a bad business for you all,' he said.

'They need to get right away from the Willows,' she said in a blunt, near aggressive tone. 'It's full of awful memories. Dad's drinking too much. They've seen a little bungalow in Wyke. They'd need every penny of the insur-

ance money as a down payment. They don't earn enough
to handle a big mortgage.'

He glanced at her as they passed between the row of
identical red-brick houses and the line of kerb-side cars.
She was flushed, looking straight ahead. 'Couldn't you
have talked them out of hiring me then?'

'Couldn't *you*? Told them it was bloody pointless?'
They'd halted at Crane's Megane, shoehorned between a
Lada and an Escort, both years old. 'You don't look as if
you're desperate for the money.' Her glance took in his car.

'I think you know as well as I do that if I turned them
down they'd go to someone else, and there's no one as
experienced as me in the city.'

'You think no end of yourself, don't you?'

'I know I'm good, yes,' he said shortly.

She flushed again, looked away. 'You know they've fed
you a load of crap, don't you?'

'Tell me about it.'

'There's no point starting the sodding job if you believe
anything *they* say about her.'

'Get in the car and give me your version then.'

'I just want you to turn them down,' she snapped. 'Let
the poor devils buy their bungalow and get away from this
dump.'

'Are you getting in the car or not?' he said bluntly.

Biting her bottom lip, she got in. Sitting behind the
wheel, Crane said, 'Look, I'd turn them down if I didn't
think they'd go to another PI who'd take the money and
do half a job. I can do without this hassle. I'll do them a no
frills job but this kind of work never comes cheap.'

She sat in sullen silence, gazing with unfocused eyes
along a street just beginning to edge into twilight. Crane

sensed an old envy she couldn't shake off. She was plain, her sister had been a stunner, even going by the grainy newspaper pictures he remembered. He glanced at her face again. She had decent bone structure, but that was it, beneath the frightful hairdo and thick coating of make-up. Maybe she'd come into her own a bit more when she was older. A mature comeliness. Even if she did he didn't think it would be much comfort to her, not whenever she thought of her sister. Dying young had meant she'd be a stunner for ever.

'She asked for it, Frank,' she said at last in a low voice.

'You could say that about plenty of young women, provocatively dressed, when the clubs start to empty. It excuses nothing.'

'You know why Joe Hellewell kept her on at Leaf and Petal? She didn't know one plant from another, not even when she'd been there six months. I'd have done anything for a chance like that. He kept her on because they fancied her rotten, the old married men the wives trailed round. If they *had* to go to a bleeding garden centre they'd go to the one Donna was at, with her big come-on smiles. She loved it. That's why he kept her on through the winter, when no bugger goes. Apart from wanting to get into her knickers himself, nasty creep.' Her voice rasped with grievance, but Crane had found that that was how the real truth often came wrapped.

'You're saying she hadn't a genuine future there?'

'She only had a future till Hellewell got his eye on someone else. He wasn't keeping her on for what she knew about flowers, that's for sure, as she couldn't tell a dahlia from a frigging geranium.'

'This Clive Fletcher—'

'Well, you know what *he's* all about, don't you? Starts off with glamour pics for the catalogues and magazines and then it's why not just one or two with your tits showing, darling, and then it's skinflicks, right?'

'Go on.'

'There's only ever him and the girl there when he tries it on. And if they give him the nod he gets the camcorder going. He pays well, so they keep their traps shut. And he tells them that if anything gets out about it they'd better start worrying about their looks.'

'How do you know all this?'

'You get it together. You pick up the whispers at the Goose.'

'You told DS Benson about it?'

She shook her head. 'Clive's respectable, what you can see of the evil swine. He does normal things most of the time: babies, weddings, family groups. Mam and Dad were always there when Mr Benson was asking about Donna's contacts. I didn't want them to hear any rumours she might be into ...' She let the sentence dangle.

'Do *you* think she was? Nude photos, porn videos?'

'No. I think he wanted to try for the straight stuff first. I honestly think he felt he could get her face going big time. If they've already done nudies, the agencies don't want to know. *I* think he thought if that didn't work he could get her into the other stuff later.'

'But you're not sure she wasn't already into the other stuff?'

'No. She was really, really secretive, even with me, though we always got on all right. She liked the smackeroonies. Clothes, jewellery, the latest mobile. She had a nice little Mini. It wasn't too old but she was sick for a convertible.'

'These other blokes that Mahon thought she was two-timing with ...'

'He wasn't wrong. She liked posh restaurants and Bobby couldn't afford them. Not with being on the Social and what he could make pushing.'

'Why bother with a bloke who'd take a swing at her?'

She sighed, shrugged. 'You tell me, with looks like she had. And Bobby wasn't all bad. He'd come to the house with flowers now and then, fill her tank, pay for repairs when he had the bread. But Donna could aggravate a bloody saint. Forget what *they* say. I've heard her and Bobby rowing. She could latch on to all those things you didn't want to hear about yourself, the things that really, really bug you. She'd throw that cruddy family in his face, and how no one would ever give a dork like him a decent job, and what a total arsehole he looked with the pony-tail. And Bobby would take it for long enough, take it for a bloody sight longer than most of the blokes round here, and then she'd go that bit too far and he'd lash out. Funny,' she said then in an almost musing tone, 'she seemed to get off on it.'

Crane watched her. She'd summed up the relationship with skill. What woman would have risked Donna's kind of looks with a man she knew she could provoke to violence unless she was hooked on the dangerous thrill? Perhaps that was how she'd liked to live her life: on the edge, taking chances, tempting fate. Perhaps she really had asked for it, death at Tanglewood.

Tears suddenly began to well along her eyelids. She shook her head irritably. 'Christ, I'm so *sick* of it,' she said, in a low harsh voice. 'Donna, Donna, bloody *Donna*! It was always her when she was alive and it's just the same now she's dead. She had everything, every mortal thing: looks, blokes, jobs, anything she wanted. And me and Marvin, we could forget it. If they'd given *us* a bit more attention I know we'd have done better. Know what I've been this last four years? A bloody checkout. That's about all I'm good for. And whoever looked at me when she was around?'

The bitter tears made her eyeliner run, which had done nothing for her looks anyway. Crane reluctantly put a hand on hers. He felt he'd coped with enough emotion for one night. But he was learning things from her he guessed he'd not get from others. And he felt sorry for the poor, blokeless kid with the tousled hair and the plain Jane looks who, life being the callous bastard it was, had given her Donna for a sister.

'I loved her *too*,' she whimpered. 'God's honest truth. Even though she had everything and I had sod all. She was such a pretty baby. I think Mam and Dad couldn't figure out how people who looked like them could have had someone who looked like her. I'd help to push her buggy and dress her and play with her. We were always together. It was when she began to grow up. She changed. When the blokes came sniffing around. I told her to go canny, over and over, she could get herself into serious bother. She just thought I was putting the mockers on. Maybe I was, a lot of the time. I still loved her but there were times when I hated her as well. God, I've felt so guilty since. That's why I can't bring myself to knock poor Bobby like they do, even if he did do it.'

'Don't take on Patsy.' He gave her hand a squeeze. 'That's what families are like, nearly all of them, and I've been involved with dozens. It's all hate and love and loyalty and guilt. You know what they say: you can choose your friends but you have to make do with the family you're given.'

Benson was sitting at the bar when Crane got there, smoking as usual and sipping a half of bitter. Dave, behind the bar, didn't need to be told to set up a gin and tonic for Crane.

'I was with the Jacksons last evening.'

Benson nodded. They got on a little better these days, but Crane knew the Donna Jackson business was going to cause resentment. Knew why and to some extent could sympathize. 'Yes, well,' he said, 'they'll not let it go, and if they're hell-bent on using a private man it had better be you.'

'I just wish they didn't have to break into their bit of savings.'

Benson sighed. 'We wanted a result on Donna more than anything we did last year, well, you've seen what decent people the Jacksons are, salt of the earth. But we got nowhere and neither will you, Frank. That's not sour grapes.'

But it was, partly. Crane said, 'Why did it take this youngster to find the body? Surely strollers must have seen it? In summer, vertical sunlight?'

'Too murky. That's why they don't want kids swimming in it. You can only see clearly for five or six feet. It must be ten, twelve deep.'

'Just how was the body weighted?'

'Plastic sack, full of biggish stones.'

'Does that mean he'd taken the stones with him? Which would mean it wasn't a spur of the moment thing.'

'No, there were plenty of stones available. There are two reservoirs at Tanglewood, yes? One above and beyond the other. Well, they buttress the banks at the sluice-way end of each reservoir with tons of stones, all a nice handy size. So we don't think it needed to be premeditated. He'd probably need to go back to his car for the sack to put the stones in and the cord to attach the sack to the body, but plenty of blokes carry stuff like that around in the boot.'

'Agreed, but if he throttled her on the spur of the moment he showed plenty of presence of mind in getting shot of the body. She *was* strangled, I seem to remember?'

Benson nodded grudgingly. He didn't much like any of this, but he reported to Terry Jones, and Terry Jones would have told him to tell Crane anything he wanted to know. 'They can prove that, if nothing else. Her being in the water for three months did nothing for the forensics. You're right, he did know how to use his noddle in a tight situation. But the low life we had in the frame could have scored on both counts. Capable of losing it and doing her in *and* finding the bottle to make a fair fist of getting shot of the body.'

'We're talking Bobby Mahon?'

'We know it's him. We both know most homicides are by people connected to the victim: lovers, spouses, offspring, neighbours. He fits the pattern like a wet T-shirt. Known to be crazy jealous and too handy with the dukes. We've seen everyone else that Donna knew that we could trace, but none of them had reason to be with her at Tanglewood the night she went missing and they all had alibis anyway.'

'Where does Mahon say he was?'

'At home, breaking out the six-packs. And his mum, his

dad and three of his mates were breaking them out with him, and they all give him the get out.'

'So they're all lying?'

'We're talking people who are never in. And on a Saturday? Do me a favour. And with his dad being that evil, lying scrote *Dougie* Mahon—'

'Not Dougie the Fence?'

'See what I mean? And Myrtle Mahon, she does her pocket money tricks on Saturdays. Can you see *her* in the house Saturday night playing knock-out whist? Well, we can't put the bugger inside without any kind of evidence, but we know it's him. I didn't say this, but we stopped looking for anyone else months ago. But no one on the Willows thinks it was anyone but Mahon. Not just us.'

'Late evening,' Crane said, 'the gays drift into the reservoir area. Did you give any of them a shake? One of them might have seen Mahon.'

'Christ, you were in the force. They're like the toms, blind, deaf and dumb unless it concerns one of their own. They don't even admit to going there, not to us. Apart from that they do their cruising on the upper level. The kid was dumped on the lower.'

Crane felt like sighing but didn't. Benson would love any sign of how impossible he felt it was to wring any more from a case a bunch of skilled policemen and women had given up on so long ago. 'You want another drink, Ted?'

'Best not. Said I'd try and be in early tonight. The kids ...'

One day, maybe they would buy each other drinks as they'd done in the past, and only then would Crane know their old close friendship was genuinely on the mend. He said, 'I had a private word with Patsy Jackson last night. She mentioned a Marvin.'

'The brother. Comes between Patsy and Donna age-wise. He has a very nice dark suit he wears for court appearances.'

'He's done time?'

'Burglary, more than one conviction. He mixes with the Dougie Mahon mob too. The rotten apple in the Jackson barrel, the others are as straight as a stick.'

'And he doesn't figure in any of this? Wouldn't *he* know where Bobby really was that night if he's in bed with the Mahons?'

'We don't think so. We had him in, Christ, we had half the Willows in. But he wasn't at the Mahons that night and checks out, and the Mahons aren't pretending he was one of the ones who was. There's nowhere to go, Frank.'

Crane wasn't prepared to agree, not if he was going to take the Jacksons' money. 'Donna herself, Ted. Patsy reckoned she might already have been living a dodgy life.'

'We're certain she was putting it about, but no definite proof. I mean, he's seriously bad news that photography bloke, Clive Fletcher. We know he's into video filth, but we can't prove that either, and that's another story. As far as Donna goes, he checks out. But we got bad vibes about her, felt she might have been her own worst enemy.'

It was the second time Crane had heard similar words. 'What about Hellewell? Leaf and Petal man?'

Benson said, 'He seemed kosher. Good looker. I reckon he had the hots for her. He wasn't alone, not by a long shot. But he looked to be in a stable marriage and his story for where he was that night's as tight as a crab's arse.' He stubbed out his final cigarette, prepared to go. 'Do you know Geoff Anderson?'

'*Standard*'s crime reporter? Took over from old Harold? The Jacksons mentioned him.'

'He gave it the column inches. It was a story that had everything going for it anyway, but he was like a dog with a bone. He's young, bright, very ambitious. *Sharp* – he couldn't have been more than five minutes behind us at the SOC.'

'How could he manage that?'

'He sweet-talks the WPCs into dropping him the word. Charm the knickers off a Carmelite nun. Anyway, he lived and breathed the story. Can't be faulted for following it up either. Rings every week: any developments?'

'The Jacksons think it might help to have a word with him.'

'He went into the background of everyone involved with a toothcomb. What he doesn't know about the Jackson killing isn't worth knowing.'

'I'll look him up.'

'All the best,' Benson said flatly. 'All you need to do is break Mahon's alibi.'

Crane was to remember those words before very long with a wry smile.

The *Standard*'s library was both state-of-the-art and user friendly. There was a small room where people wanting to study back numbers could sit at a VDU undisturbed.

Crane was rapidly able to key to the relevant editions, scroll through the pages and bring up the reports on Donna's death. He started with the front page splash, when Liam Patterson, the underwater swimmer, had touched first a plastic bag that seemed full of something hard and uneven, which was connected by a cord to something soft and smooth. 'DONNA'S BODY FOUND', the headline blared.

A body was discovered in the lower of the Tanglewood reservoirs, a well-known local beauty spot, and has been identified as that of Donna Jackson missing from home for three months. The discovery was made by an eleven-year-old boy swimming in the reservoir, despite being forbidden to do so on many occasions by rangers. The police, while taking a strong line on this dangerous practice, admit that in this case it has enabled them, however tragically, to bring their long, dedicated search for Donna to an end. They can reveal that they are to begin immediately re-interviewing everyone known to have been in contact with her, and are optimistic of being able to make an early arrest of the person responsible for the savage killing of this pretty and popular young woman ...

There was a quarter-page photo of Donna Jackson's face. The expert lighting and technique indicated professionalism. Maybe the man called Fletcher had taken it. She really had been incredibly attractive. Smooth, silky, shoulder-length hair in a highlighted honey colour, perfect regular teeth, a small, well-shaped nose, big round eyes that would have seemed luminous even without a key light. The eyes riveted. They seemed to hint at an odd soulful quality, a refinement, an innocence even, that seemed well out of synch with what Crane was beginning to learn about her. He held an old envelope over the left side of her face, then transferred it to the right. Each side seemed a perfect, near geometrical match for the other. He'd read that this precision of feature in an already attractive woman was an extra subliminal turn-on for men.

The man he kept hearing about, Geoff Anderson, was bylined at the head of the report, and on the ones that followed. They became briefer as the search for the killer went on, and though a man was reported to be 'helping the police with their enquiries', no other reference was made to him.

Earlier reports, those published when Donna had simply been missing, included interviews Anderson had had with the Jacksons, plus several with various of Donna's friends and work mates. He'd described her more than once as a high-spirited and outgoing eighteen-year-old with dazzling looks, who was highly regarded at the Leaf and Petal garden centre, and quite possibly on the verge of a brilliant career as a fashion model. She liked to be out and about a lot, but had never been in any kind of trouble and had always been seen at home as an ideal and much-loved daughter and sister.

Crane sat back sceptically. It was all too anodyne. He'd been given the impression Anderson had his ear to the ground. The young woman he was writing about could have been any one of the bright kids you could see most nights in the city pubs and clubs. But there'd been a darker side to Donna Jackson. A Donna who was streetwise and needed no lessons in pulling the men. A Donna who seemed to have a dangerous fascination for being handed a bunch of fives. No hint of any of that in Anderson's reports, though he was said to have researched her background intensively. Could that mean he'd taken Connie and Malc's rose-tinted view of their younger daughter at face value? A crime reporter supposed to have a hard nose?

'I'd not read on. They never do get their man.' Crane turned around. 'Geoff Anderson, Mr Crane. I saw your name in the book. I've heard quite a bit about you.'

Crane gave a crooked smile. 'None of it good, I daresay.'

'Terry Jones always speaks very highly of you.'

'Until my spot of trouble, yes, I know.'

Crane didn't want to talk about it and Anderson could tell. He perched on the edge of a side table. He looked to be mid-twenties and had fair wavy hair, dark blue eyes, a bluntish nose and a full wide mouth. He was strongly built and near six foot but carried no extra weight. He wore a pale blue poplin shirt, open at the neck, fawn woollen trousers and brown loafers.

'I don't see a man in your line looking up the Donna Jackson story out of idle curiosity,' Anderson said, smiling.

'I was aiming to contact you, Geoff. Connie and Malc, you obviously know them well, have hired me and want me to see if I can turn up anything new about the killing.'

'About Bobby Mahon?'

'Everyone's keen to write his name on the charge sheet.'

He shrugged. 'He's not helped himself. If he's innocent why not admit where he really was the night she disappeared? He certainly wasn't at home playing three-card brag. I had a go at them myself, Mahon's pals. Were they really at his place that night? I had a go at the neighbours: brick wall. They said that if the Mahons *said* they were at home that night they were at home, wherever they really were. On the Willows no one messes with the Mahons. But if they weren't at home where were they, especially master Bobby? Nowhere I could find out.'

'You really have given it a lot of time,' Crane said evenly, not wanting to give any hint of the frustration the case was already giving him.

'The story had legs. A local *cause célèbre*. Just about everyone on the Willows knew her, because of those incredible looks. It was like someone had killed a rare butterfly. It got everyone worried about their own teenage daughters, in case the killer struck again.'

'Knew her yourself?'

He shook his head. 'I'd seen her around. I trawl the scene: the pubs, the clubs, the casinos. You couldn't miss her, seemed to be everywhere. You should have seen her, strutting her stuff with the strobes flickering on her hair. Out of this world. Why do you ask?'

Crane gave him a steady look. 'It seems to me you've

written her up like the girl next door. I've already picked up that that wasn't the case.'

He gave Crane a wry grin. 'You're right, it wasn't. She had a taste for the wild side. Could have been doing flesh-market photos for Fletcher, if not worse, we'll never know for sure. I'm pretty certain she was screwing around, probably for the loot, but no punter's going to come forward and put his hand up. On top of that, she played her cards incredibly close, so close even her pals didn't really know what she was up to, even if they had a bloody good idea.'

'Why not write some of that up, or at least hint at it? She certainly wasn't helping herself to stay out of trouble.'

Anderson watched him in a brief silence. 'The wench was dead, Frank, and I'd spent a *lot* of time with Connie and Malc. They had such a shed-load of misery on their backs I felt it would finish them off if there was any hint their beautiful girl was less than perfect. I couldn't prove anything, it was all hints and murmurs, after all, so I wrote her up as they wanted her to be seen. You're looking cynical.' He smiled in the engaging way he had. Crane guessed it must have got him across many a hostile doorstep.

He said, 'When did a seasoned reporter ever worry too much what anyone thought if he believed he was telling the truth?'

Anderson shook his head, still smiling. 'You don't miss too many tricks do you? All right, I left out the dodgy bits. And why, because the editor wanted it that way, and he said the public wanted it that way. You've seen her picture, *no one* wanted to believe that that innocent-looking slip of a kid was anything other than she seemed. The killing was

29

big local news. It was also a circulation booster. So I didn't bend the truth, I just left bits out. We call it editing.'

'And that's why you're so keen for a result? Another circulation boost? Benson says you follow it up on a weekly basis.'

The reporter was again silent for a short time. 'Between you and me, Frank,' he said finally, 'I see London as my next career move, working for one of the nationals. Sounds a bit of a cliché, I know. And whether Donna's killer's nailed or not, I'm aiming to write the big one, the in-depth feature about Donna's life and times. The Willows is falling apart and we know why: unemployment, broken homes, drugs, teenage pregnancies, apathy. The situation with the inner cities has been written up endlessly. Well, I want my feature to be based on Donna's short tragic life. Donna will symbolize the Willows' decline and the Willows in the end destroying one of its rarest possessions. Even if it wasn't Mahon who killed her, I'm certain her fate was dictated by her environment. I want this article to touch the spot, maybe even taken up and syndicated. It could do wonders for my CV.'

Crane nodded. That had to be the real reason he'd not wanted to write up Donna as a streetwise tramp, or even hint at it. He needed an apparently artless innocent to contrast with the slum the Willows was becoming. Journalists were an odd breed. He accepted that they had feelings like everyone else, yet people's tragedies were their livelihood and their ambitions were based on them. Though Crane had to remind himself that he also was using Donna's fate as his own livelihood, if not a welcome change from routine.

'Did you have any dealings with Mahon?' he asked.

'I talked to him when they let him go. Asked him about their relationship and whether he suspected anyone himself. Tried to catch him out. Fat chance, if two bobbies hammering away couldn't break his story. He just banged on about it not being him, he'd been at home, the same old bullshit. Near to tears at times.'

'I'd heard he could get emotional.'

'You aim to see him yourself?'

'I'll have to. If I can't break that alibi of his I can forget it. He just might *not* be guilty, but there's no point in looking any further until I know for certain. Where do I find him? The Goose and Guinea?'

'I'll go with you, if you like. He's always there early doors, except when he's sitting quietly at home the one night his girlfriend ends up at the bottom of a reservoir.'

Crane's instinct was to turn him down. He worked alone and Anderson could be a distraction. On the other hand, it might help if the ice was broken with Mahon by someone who knew him. 'You can find the time?'

'No problem. Mahon might think he's off the hook now. Could give him a nice little turn, me drifting back into his life with a PI.'

The sort of turn that might just get him to let something slip.

'Free this evening?'

'Unless something comes up between now and then. I'll contact you.'

'Thanks a lot.' Crane gave him his card, gave a final glance at the VDU, then cleared the screen. 'I'm finished here.'

They walked from the library and halted at the top of the steps, Crane to leave, Anderson to return to the big open-plan office he shared with the other journalists, from where the soft endless sound of phone bells could just be heard.

'Look,' Anderson said, 'there's not much I haven't ferreted out about Donna and who she knew. I'll do anything I can to help. And, like you, I don't work nine to five.'

'I'll bear that in mind,' Crane said evenly, still not keen to get too involved with a reporter who would very much have his own agenda. At the same time, he had to admit that Anderson was sitting on gold-plated information it would take him hours to put together himself.

They stood on the balcony overlooking the reception area. A sepia-tinted wall of glass encased the ultra modern complex and silent cars and buses seemed to float along the road below, their windows and brightwork flashing in the afternoon sun. 'It's not just the brownie points, Frank,' Anderson said, as if he'd sensed what Crane had been thinking earlier. 'I really did feel sorry about the kid. We all did. She wasn't a very nice girl, but I honestly think she was a victim of her background. The Willows has a lot to answer for.'

Just then, three young women came out of the open-plan room, all prettyish and cheerful looking. 'Geoff, you're back?' one of them said. 'Now you see him, now you don't. You are coming to the Tav, aren't you?'

'Darlings, how *could* I refuse?' he said, giving them his peculiarly endearing smile. Apart from being good looking he was also fanciable, going by the way they clustered round him. Crane knew the two things didn't always go together. One of the women, who had green eyes, rosy cheeks and black curly hair, was clearly mad about the bloke.

'All right,' she said, 'see you there then, and if anything should pop up let's hope it's nothing to do with work.'

'Saucy....'

They went off giggling, the dark-haired one turning back for a last glance.

'Tell you what,' Anderson said, still grinning faintly, 'it's a custom here, meeting up at the Tavern, whoever's around, about six. Your office is in the Old Quarter, why not drop in? I'll know by then if I'm free and we can go on to the Goose.'

The Tavern occupied the ground floor of what had once been a wool warehouse. It had become known as the Glass-house. There was glass everywhere, along the walls and the bar facings. The tables were glass, the chandeliers dripped shards of it, partitions had frosted glass panels. It drew a young crowd.

Eight or nine people sat at one of the oblong central tables when Crane walked in, and he could hear the rapid gun fire of Anderson's voice. 'Some things just are,' he was saying. 'There's no rational explanation, they just *are*. Why are women called Dawn always overweight and have badly bleached hair? Have you ever known a man called Bernard to be entirely right in the head? Have you ever been able to watch any film that had heart in the title? See what I mean?'

'How about wind?' Crane said from behind him. 'I have the same trouble with films that have wind in the title. *Gone with the* being the exception that proves the rule.'

'Frank!' He jumped to his feet. 'Let me get you a drink. This is Frank Crane, folks, and we're helping each other on a piece of work. What are you drinking, pal?'

He went off to the bar and the others smiled and nodded. Crane recognized one or two of the faces from the little photos that went with their bylines at the top of articles on education and entertainment and community affairs.

'Your face rings some kind of a bell.' It was the woman with the black curly hair Crane had seen earlier. The seat he'd taken was next to hers.

'I'm ex-police,' he told her, 'and now working as a PI. I've been involved in a recent high profile case that got my face in your paper, though I try very hard to keep it out.'

'I see. I'm Carol. What are you two cooperating on?'

'Donna Jackson, yes? Her people have hired me to see if I can turn up anything new on the killer. Geoff has a lot of useful information.'

She sighed, her eyes leaving Crane's to rest on Anderson's lean form where he stood at the bar. 'I might have known.' She looked back at him. 'They've all got one, you know,' she said ruefully. 'Crime reporters. An outsize bee in the bonnet. There's always one that's insoluble and causes a hell of a stir that they'll never let go. There are crime reporters with grey hair and paunches who are still hell-bent on tracing Lord Lucan, for God's sake, and he's been declared officially *dead*.'

Crane shrugged. 'I'm sure you're right, but his information is valuable to me if he's willing to share it.'

'Oh, Donna *Jackson* …'

Crane seemed to hear an echo of Patsy's voice when they'd sat in his car. Maybe Anderson had given so much time to the story that Carol had begun to feel very neglected. Assuming she was his girlfriend.

Then she gave him a little impish grin. 'You'll have to watch him, you know, our Geoff. He's a great guy, but he tends to take over and run things. He's also got a clever line in implying his information gathering was more than useful in bringing certain villains to a court room.'

He watched her. None of that worried him much. He'd be working alone on the Jackson case, whatever Anderson imagined, with this single exception of going with him to see Mahon. He'd already sensed his nuisance value, having had experience of handling reporters from his days in the force, when flawed reporting at the wrong moment could damage a sensitive investigation. All he wanted from Anderson was what he knew, and as far as he was concerned, if Donna's killer was ever found, the reporter could then claim all the glory going. Crane was a man who's anonymity was crucial to the work he did.

He knew Anderson was back by the way Carol's grin suddenly ignited into a warm smile. 'There you go, Frank,' Anderson said, putting down a gin and tonic in front of him. 'Any amusing deaths, you guys, as Bowra used to say?' he said to the others. 'Any juicy bits of scandal among the city fathers? I'm picking up a rumour from a London chum who reckons a heavily married Blair Babe is finding her way to the pied-à-terre of a heavily married junior minister on a career path. He thinks they sit in the dark when they're not playing gee-gees in the dark. Now who does that remind you of?'

Fifteen minutes passed, with Anderson's rapid delivery keeping them amused and intrigued by turns. Apart from being attractive to women he seemed also to be very much a man's man. It was the engaging smile, the hand that briefly touched an arm. He was also a good listener, despite being so irrepressible himself. He had charm in spades. Crane distrusted charm, as it could have an ugly side when it didn't work, but he had to admit that in Anderson's game it was virtually essential.

'Are you free tonight, Geoff?' Carol said, at a brief pause in the animated chat. 'There's *The Constant Gardener* showing at the Odeon. Fancy a bite at Frère Antoine's and catching the second house?'

'Carol, beloved, I should have explained. I'm going on somewhere from here with Frank. Another night, yes?'

'Right you are,' she said, with a brightness that didn't quite cover what Crane could tell was intense disappointment.

'Let's go then, Frank. Chummy should now be ensconced. My car's in Vicar Lane so I'll see you up there in about fifteen, OK?'

The Goose and Guinea had been built when the Willows was being developed in the late 1930s. It ran catty-cornered to the main road and at the end of the estate's principal drive. Apart from being dated it also had no style. Built of shiny, yellowish brick, it had a flat roof, odd, rounded corners and long, narrow, metal-framed windows. It had a dubious reputation but was well run, mainly because the landlord was built like a medium-sized wardrobe.

They went in and Crane bought drinks. The pub was open-plan, with an annexe at the rear in which a few young T-shirted men played pool. Another man sat watching them gloomily.

'Mahon's the one sitting. Must have been played out. That's handy. Let's go sit with him.'

Crane followed him across the main room, quiet at present, to the banquette seating beyond the table.

'Hello, Bobby. Thought I might find you here. Mind if we join you for a few minutes? How are you doing these days, old son?'

Crane had to hand it to him, his manner with a possible killer was exactly as warm as it had been with his colleagues at the Glass-house. Mahon peered slightly in the gloom that surrounded the sharp even glare of the pool table's canopied lamps.

'Oh, it's you,' he said flatly.

'This is Frank Crane, Bobby. He's a very skilled private investigator. Malc and Connie have engaged him to see if he can throw any light on Donna's murder, seeing as the police have got nowhere.'

Mahon gave an indifferent nod. 'So 'e can try and prove it was me?' he muttered. 'That's why they've taken 'im on. Malc and Connie never thought it was no one else.'

'I've got an open mind, Bobby,' Crane said quietly. 'I doubt there'll be much the police missed. I'm just going to take a fresh look and talk to the people who knew her.'

'No good talking to me, mister. I don't know *nothing* about that murder. I only wish I did. The police never stopped trying to pin it on me, even though I were sat at 'ome with me mates.'

On an instinct, both Crane and Anderson let the silence roll, in the hope that it might encourage Mahon to say something, anything else that might give them a lead. But Mahon seemed sunk in apathy. He had pale blue eyes and thick fair hair scraped back from his forehead in the pony-tail Donna had been so scathing about. It was knotted by a narrow blue ribbon, a grotesquely demure touch. He had a broad nose and thick lips that gave him a slightly feral appearance, though it didn't detract from his roughish good looks. He was strongly built and wore a T-shirt of an unattractive shade of green, faded jeans and black moccasin boots. He had what the police tended to call a 'building site' tan.

Finally breaking the silence, he said in a low voice, 'You don't know what it's like.'

'What's that, Bobby?' Anderson asked in a kindly tone.

'No fucker believing you. Not just the police, they never believe no one. It's Connie and Malc and them.'

'It can be very upsetting. I've talked to an awful lot of people who've had the same problem. They've got a perfectly honest alibi but because they knew the victim so well it gets the Chinese whispers going.'

'I didn't *feel* good that night, Geoff. I wasn't up for it, getting a few down in 'ere and then doing the clubs. I'd come over all shivery. I told the lads I was 'aving a night in, so they said they'd 'ave one as well, we'd play some poker.'

Mahon's words sounded rehearsed even now, a year on. Crane wondered how many times he'd recited them to the police. He found it impossible to believe that the sort of men Mahon knocked about with would sacrifice a Saturday night out because a mate had come over all shivery.

Crane spoke in as sympathetic a tone as Anderson's. 'These things happen, Bobby. I don't suppose it helped much that your mum and dad had decided to stay in too that night.'

'Me mam were worried about me! I'm never sick. I only wish they 'ad gone out. Folk wouldn't keep saying we'd all 'ad our 'eads together.'

Crane had expected to find a Mahon who'd be intensely

guarded, if not hostile, but he seemed to want to talk, if only to justify himself. His friends would have heard enough, months ago, about the Donna killing, and probably wouldn't listen any more. And maybe Mahon still wanted to talk so compulsively he was even ready to make do with him and Anderson.

'Look, Bobby,' Crane said, 'I'd be really grateful for any help you could give me. You know who Donna's contacts were. You must have your own suspicions?'

His pale blue eyes moodily met Crane's. 'Never trusted that arsehole she worked for. Leaf and Petal bloke. Seemed fond to me, know what I mean? Kept 'er on that winter. I thought aye aye, 'cause she knew fuck all about plants and that. They 'ad a Christmas do and I picked 'er up. Didn't like the way 'e was eyeballing 'er in that tight dress. Fond. I could 'ave flattened the bugger.'

'You think he might have been trying to get off with her?'

'Sure of it. Mind you,' he said dolefully, 'who wasn't with Donna?' His eyes had a haunted look in the smoky dimness.

'Trouble is, Bobby, Joe Hellewell's alibi's rock solid, just like yours,' Anderson pointed out in his friendly way.

'Fletcher then. I told 'er time and again not to 'ave nothing to do with the slimy sod.'

'Same problem there, old son. The police cleared him.'

Crane said, 'Bobby, I don't want to upset you more than I have to, but do you think it's possible Donna *was* seeing someone else on a regular basis? She was quite young, wasn't she? Maybe she didn't feel ready for a settled relationship.'

'That's what all the bother were about, weren't it?' he

broke out. 'Er seeing other blokes behind me back. All right, I 'ad a one-night-stand now and then, didn't I, but that's different, innit?'

Crane knew it was, in the male dinosaur climate of the Willows. 'Do you know who any of these blokes might have been? It could be very important.'

'She'd never let on to me, mister. She were always so close. She thought I'd go and put 'em in 'ospital. Too right.'

'It must have made you very cross, Bobby,' Anderson said mildly, in his deceptively leading way.

Mahon looked irritably from one to the other of them. 'I didn't 'it 'er 'cause of that,' he said shortly. 'That's what *they* tried to make out, that I knocked 'er about 'cause of the two-timing. Well, I never. I only 'it 'er two or three times and that was 'cause she wound me up rotten. You don't know what she could be like: said I weren't going nowhere and me family were crap and me wheels should be on the tip and ... and ...' He broke off, reddening. Crane guessed she'd probably jeered at his sexual technique too. If she'd slept around she'd be able to make value judgements. He felt no sympathy for a man who'd knock a woman about, but Mahon was only saying what Patsy had said, that Donna had had a fatal instinct for picking on all those things about yourself you least wanted to hear.

He caught Anderson's eye, shrugged. They were getting nowhere. Crane didn't even have an instinct about Mahon's innocence or guilt. Bobby came from a criminal background, that was the trouble. It put him ahead of the game when it came to lying his way out of things, including murder. Yet for once in a blue moon he just could have been at home on a Saturday night and had the bad luck to choose a blue moon night when his girlfriend's body was hitting the bottom of a reservoir.

'Well, thanks for your help, Bobby,' he said politely. 'And I really am very sorry about Donna.'

'We'll let you get on with your pool,' Anderson added. 'Where's Cliff, by the way? Unusual not to see you two together.'

That seemed to leave him even more depressed. 'Don't know,' he muttered. "aven't seen 'im in weeks.'

'Don't say you've had a bust up with your best friend on top of everything else?'

Mahon took out a cigarette and lit it from a disposable lighter with a trembling hand. He sat slumped on the banquette, gazing with unfocused eyes over the pool table, where the others were chalking the tips of their cues and sipping from fresh pints.

'Coming in, Bobby mate?'

He shook his head. 'Next frame, Heppo.'

As the balls began clicking again, he suddenly started to cry, the tears rapidly welling and trickling down his tanned cheeks. He looked to be in a state of total despair, and maybe he was, but Crane knew from long experience that guilty men could weep just as bitterly as the innocent.

'You don't know what it's like,' he said once more, in a thin mewing tone. 'All of 'em, the 'ole bleeding Willows, looking at you like you was shit. Crossing the street when they see you coming. Reckoning you're not there. People you've known all your fucking life. Mrs Bateson ... she were like a nana to me once, last week she *spit* at me! None of the totty'll go near me, I'm that bad news. It gets round the clubs and them bitches won't even *dance* with me, let alone ...'

Crane thought, who could blame them? The story would be about that if you glanced at another man Bobby gave you a mouthful of signet rings and if you went out with one he topped you. And this would have gone on since Donna's body had been winched up nine months ago. No wonder he seemed near-suicidal.

Anderson touched Mahon's arm. 'We know how you're feeling, Bobby. We've seen it all. People can be very unfair. The police have cleared you, why won't they accept it? In Australia the Aborigines call it pointing the bone. If they decide someone's done something really bad in one of their little communities they actually point a bone at him, and after that no one will have anything to do with him. He's out of it. They sometimes go off and die because they're so unhappy. It's a lousy deal, being cut off by your own people and that's what they're doing to you on the Willows. They're not even *trying* to give you a fair shake and it's just not on.'

Crane glanced at the reporter. He sounded sympathetic, but he'd managed to come up with an image that had left Mahon even more distressed. He'd gone pale, the cigarette smouldering between stained fingers. He wondered if this was the flip side of the Anderson charm. He'd spent untold hours on the story, maybe he was convinced it could only be Mahon. And if Mahon wasn't going in front of a jury, why not rub it in that the jury of the Willows wouldn't be a soft touch?

'I didn't *do* it, Geoff,' he gasped. 'I were crackers about 'er. I wanted 'er to live with me, we could 'ave put us name down for a council flat. It done me 'ead in, just clipping 'er them one or two times, I felt that bad about it. I couldn't 'ave done that carry-on at Tanglewood, *couldn't* 'ave. Christ, why won't no one *believe* me?'

The two men walked across the car park to claim their motors. Crane still wasn't entirely sure about Mahon's guilt, though he'd not known a case where the evidence for it stacked up so credibly. No wonder the police had shelved it and moved on, having made every possible check. There was an outside chance the killer was someone who'd covered his tracks too well, but if the police couldn't get Mahon out of the frame he knew they'd not look further, their resources were too limited. He said, 'Well, thanks, Geoff. At least I got the measure of the beast, if nothing else.'

'That stuff about the Abos. I thought it might loosen him up a bit, with him being already in a low state.'

'There could be a delayed reaction.' But he was certain there wouldn't be. Mahon would get over it and the Willows would get over it, because that's how life went on the estate. And for all his tears, Mahon had shown no anxiety about Crane making a fresh start on the case. That meant he either felt totally secure in his alibi, or might, just might, be as innocent as he protested he was.

Anderson peered round the car park. 'Hell, what's happened to my car?' he said. Then he tapped his forehead with the heel of his hand. 'I'm losing it. I'm in the office runabout, my wheels are in for repair.' He opened the door of an elderly Astra. 'I thought for a second one of Mahon's low life chums had nicked mine while we were talking to him. They're full of tricks like that. Keep in touch, Frank.'

Crane muttered, 'In your dreams,' as he got into his

Megane. Anderson's way with people like Mahon weren't his, though to be fair the reporter had unknowingly given him what could be a very small lead, and so the meeting with Mahon might not have been a total write off.

As Anderson drove back to the city, he knew he had to find some way of keeping tabs on Crane. He needed to know what he was up to every foot of the way and it wouldn't be easy, as Crane, being ex-CID, would be skilled in fending off crime reporters. And Crane had been one of their best. He studied the angles, thought things through, picked up clues others had missed. And if Crane could come up with anything new on the Donna Jackson story, anything at all, Anderson had to be the first to get his hands on it. There was the big feature he wanted to write, which he was certain would be crucial to his future career. His future career was never out of his mind for very long.

THREE

'Patsy?'

'That's me.'

'Frank Crane. I'd like your help. Do you know a bloke called Cliff who was a mate of Bobby Mahon's, by any chance?'

'Known him all my life. Cliff Greenwood. He lives nearby.'

'Wasn't he Bobby's best friend?'

'Never go near each other now.'

'Why's that, do you think?'

'Because Cliff thinks Bobby did for Donna, like everyone else.'

'But ... wouldn't Cliff have been one of the three friends of Bobby's who were supposed to have been at home with him that night?'

'Yes, I'd say that that must mean he *knows* Bobby wasn't where he said he was.'

'What kind of a bloke is he?'

'Cliff? He's been bad news in the past, like the others. And then he got a really decent probation bloke on his case. Talked him into starting over, got him to go back to his joinery classes. He's in the double glazing now and going straight.'

'Would that be why he split with Bobby?'

'No, they were still best mates even when Cliff started going straight. Bobby didn't hold it against him. I think he was more than a bit envious, you ask me. I sometimes think if only Bobby hadn't had Dougie and Myrtle as parents ... what chance did he have, poor sod?'

'I need to talk to Cliff, Patsy. Where does he spend his evenings?'

'He never goes near the Goose now. They say he's been seen in the Toll Gate now and then.'

'Would you do me a big favour? I daresay he'll still be at home. Could you ring him and ask him if you could see him at the Toll Gate? Tell him your mum and dad are thinking of buying that bungalow and would like an idea on cost for putting in double glazing. Then we could go together, if you wouldn't mind and you're free. I could pick you up.'

'Oh, I'll be free,' she said in a resigned tone. 'I usually am.'

The Toll Gate was old, small and cosy. It had chintzy curtains, planters and wall lamps with rose-coloured shades. It wasn't the sort of place that did pool tables. Cliff Greenwood sat gloomily over a pint of lager, as if nostalgic for pop music and the clicking of snooker balls. He was a near-clone of Mahon and his friends, except that his reddish hair was normal length and neatly combed, and he wore a newish sports jacket and twill trousers. He had a plump, slightly spotty face and grey-green eyes that watched Crane warily as he and Patsy joined him at a circular table with an ornate metal base.

'Hi, Cliff. This is a friend of mine, Frank Crane.'

He looked startled. It couldn't have done much for Patsy's morale, Crane thought, Donna's plain sister, not known for pulling the guys. Any guys.

'How do,' he said grudgingly, not offering a hand. Crane put down their drinks and they sat.

'I've got some leaflets, Patsy. They'll give Connie and Malc an idea what we do. I can give you a ballpark on price if you can tell me how many windows the bungalow's got, but I'd need to see it to give you a proper estimate.'

'Cliff,' Crane said. 'Forget the double glazing. I'm a private investigator who used to be a cop and I'm working for the Jacksons to see if I can clear up Donna's killing.'

'What's this bugger's game, Patsy?' he said tersely. 'I'm here about windows and if we're not talking windows we're talking nothing.'

'Look, Cliff,' Crane said, 'I needed to see you and I needed Patsy to vouch for me. You do *want* Donna's killing clearing up, don't you, if that's humanly possible?'

'Look, mister, I did all my talking to the real police. I'm not doing any more.' He began to swallow the rest of his pint. 'I'm out of here.'

'Cliff ...' Patsy put a hand on his arm. 'You know Mam and Dad. You know how gutted they are about Donna. They'll not rest till someone gets banged up for it. You don't need me to tell you who.'

'I know that, I know that ...' He gave an exasperated sigh. 'I'm gutted as well. We all are. She was very special. But I'm not going to *talk* about it any more.'

'The police believe you're protecting your best mate, Cliff,' Crane said evenly.

'Best *mate*!' He gave his head a single, disgusted, upward shake.

'Everyone knows you had a bust up, Cliff,' Patsy said. 'And no one really holds it against you for not grassing him, not on the Willows. They think he should have done the decent thing and owned up to where he was. No one believes you were all staying in, playing cards. You know that as well as I do.'

'Yes, well ... see you around.' He slammed down his empty glass and got up.

Crane said, 'Cliff, do you understand what perverting the course of justice means? Well, that's what they'll think you've done if Bobby really wasn't at home that night. And if it ever comes out that he wasn't they're going to lean very hard on you and the others for wasting police time. And if it comes out that Bobby really is in the frame ...'

Half turned away, he glanced back at them. 'I'll just have to take my chances then, won't I?'

'And lose the first decent job you've had in your life? And your self-respect? What do you make: four, five hundred sovs a week? Are you ready to walk away from all that?'

His round face took on a troubled look in the gathering dusk. Crane guessed he'd never allowed himself to think as far as that. Agitated, he turned away again.

'Cliff,' Crane said quietly, 'I have police contacts. They trust me. If you helped me I'd put in a good word for you. We could say you'd alibied Bobby under duress. That means you were afraid what the Mahons would do if you grassed him.'

'Christ, what do you think they'd do if I grassed him anyway?' he said, so jumpy now he wasn't guarding his words.

'They'd never know. I'd keep your name out of everything to do with them. We're not even having this little chat.'

'Cliff ...' Patsy said.

Finally, with intense reluctance, he sat down again, staring miserably into space, forehead deeply furrowed.

'Patsy, would you mind getting Cliff another lager. And another for yourself, if you like.' He gave her a ten pound note.

As she moved off, from where they sat in a corner of the small bar parlour, Crane said, 'Look ... Cliff, all I really need to know for certain is that Bobby wasn't home that night. I can take it from there. It's not worth my breaking sweat if I can't get that confirmed.'

'None of us was there,' he said at last, in a low nervous voice. 'Except Myrtle maybe. You can give her one at her place or yours, only she charges extra at her place, for the free drinks.'

'*None* of you?' Crane found it hard to stay calm.

Patsy put down the drinks, placing the change at Crane's elbow in a neat little pile. 'Sure you don't want one yourself, Frank?'

'Not just now.'

'If any of this got out ...' Greenwood's lips trembled.

'Cliff, you know you can trust *me*,' Patsy said. 'God, with a brother like Marvin never out of bother ...'

Eyes flicking from her to Crane, he finally went on. 'Dougie Mahon ... he was working on a big one that night, wasn't he? He said we didn't need to be *in* their house, but if we did go out it hadn't to be nowhere local, and we had to swear we *had* been at their place, just chance he ever got his collar felt.'

Crane sank back on the plush banquette. 'So that's it. You were really covering Dougie's backside?'

The other nodded, a look of near-panic in his eyes for what he was forcing himself to admit. 'Christ, why did she have to go and get herself topped the same night?'

'So, Bobby *couldn't* say he was anywhere else? Even if he hadn't been with Donna?'

'It was big, big,' the other man said, almost in a whisper. 'Dougie had to have a cast-iron alibi for if anything went wrong. It just meant Bobby had it too. If the two things hadn't happened together there'd not have been all this bother, would there? Bobby'd be on his own and he'd have to prove where he was.'

'But Cliff, *murder*!' Crane said. 'Surely you must have realized it had all got too big to handle?'

'No one lets Dougie Mahon down,' he said, the whites of his eyes briefly flaring. 'Not even if Bobby had put half a pound of Semtex under the town hall.'

'Did Bobby do it, Cliff?'

'He swore he hadn't. Over and over again. Even to his dad, even though he knew Dougie would never have grassed him. Dougie needed to look after his own arse and he'd always thought Donna was getting to be serious trouble anyway. He has a nose for things.'

'Do you believe Bobby?'

He shook his head despondently. 'He'd been me best mate since we were kids, but he was a born liar. Got it from Dougie.'

'Liar, liar, pants on fire. That's what they used to shout at him in the playground at school,' Patsy added.

'Why get involved in giving Dougie an alibi in the first place, Cliff? When you were trying to go straight?'

He shrugged. 'Old times' sake. They were good to me when Mam and Dad split up, treated me like one of the family. Whenever they gave Bobby pocket money they'd give me some as well. Everyone knew Dougie shifted bent gear, it didn't seem no big deal to say I was there that night.'

'How big was this big one?'

'You don't want to know.'

'Oh, come on, Cliff, there were rumours all over the Willows,' Patsy said. 'It was guns, wasn't it?'

'*Guns?*' This time Crane couldn't conceal his shock. 'God, not the IRA! There's been a ceasefire for years, they're supposed to be handing them all in.'

Greenwood gave a wry smile. 'No, not the shamrocks. Antiques. The geezer had a roomful. Dougie set it all up.'

Crane remembered now. A palatial house on the moorland fringe of the metropolitan area. A clean job, the guns carefully lifted and just as carefully disposed of. 'And Dougie was never in the frame?'

'He knew he would be if it ever came out he'd not been at home. It was the sort of scam had his dabs on, know what I mean?'

'So where were you that night, the rest of you?'

'Two of us went to a pub in Otley where they didn't know us from Elton John, played darts. Bobby ... well, he went off on his own. Said he'd been clubbing in Leeds with some French totty he'd picked up in Bradford the week before.'

'And the totty's back over the Channel now and he's no idea where she lives?'

'Doesn't even know her surname. Said they called her Nicole.'

'Nicole from France. He's going to have to do better than that. Well done, Cliff. You have my word none of this will put you in it. We'll leave you in peace now.'

He nodded unhappily. They left him hunched over his pint. He was clearly struggling to come to terms with the breaking of the only rule that counted on the Willows: you never grassed *anyone*, not ever, whoever they were, whatever they'd done.

They walked out to Crane's car; he opened the passenger door for her from the outside. She looked confused. Maybe no one had ever done that before. 'Thanks, Patsy, you've been a great help. I'll drop you at home, yes?'

'I don't live there. I stay a lot since Ronnie legged it, but I have my own place. Conway House.'

He'd once made a call at Conway House. It was a largish two storey building on the edge of the Willows. It had been built to a tight budget and had pebbledash walls and a shallow roof. There was a single communal entrance and small flats ran off both sides of end to end corridors. 'They're not much,' she said, as Crane drew up in front, 'but they're cheap. We were supposed to be saving for our own place when he took off. Fancy a drink?'

He didn't, but she spoke in such a flat, resigned tone as if certain he'd refuse, that he said, 'Thanks, I wouldn't mind.'

She looked confused again. He followed her across the narrow, paved front yard and inside. The corridor was dimly lit and carpeted in shabby grey rubber-back. The doors were painted a uniform magnolia and identified by screw-on metal numbers. The flat had four little rooms: bath, kitchen, living and bed, and overlooked a poorly tended oval of lawn and half a dozen garages in need of repainting, lit by a single overhead lamp.

'You have to be here five years to get near one of those,' she said. 'Ronnie used to go bananas. He thought more of that broken down Escort than he ever did of me and it had fifty thousand on when he bought the bloody thing.'

He sounded to be a true son of the Willows. But she'd furnished the living room imaginatively in a mail order sort of way, with tab-top curtains in a cheerful check, a plain green carpet, a metal-framed uplighter and ceramic table lamps. There was a tiny three piece and a small dining table with upholstered chairs. 'Nice place,' he said.

She coloured slightly. 'Glad you like it. Ronnie was all for using things from his mam's till we could afford a mortgage. I told him you'd have to pay someone to take them to the tip. Do you want G and T, like in the pub?'

'A small one.'

She went in the galley kitchen. Crane took off his jacket and stood at the window. Poor kid. In Donna's shadow most of her life and then Ronnie, fonder of an old banger than of her. But Crane knew his own reasons for taking a drink with her couldn't be looked at too closely. He felt sorry for her but he also needed her input. She'd made a first class job of fixing the meeting with Greenwood, and her inside knowledge of what really went on on the Willows couldn't be bettered. She was a valuable contact. Story of her life: being used.

He gave a crooked grin. If only she'd ditch the ghastly hairdo and the garish make-up. She was a plain woman and whatever she did with her looks she would never have any of the kind of glamour her sister had been given in spades, at birth. He still felt maturity would bring its own reward. Maybe one day she'd wake up and realize she'd never be able to compete with Donna's ghost, and she'd look better for being herself. And if that brought her any kind of self-confidence, well that went a lot further than looks anyway.

'There you go,' she said, handing him his drink. 'Glad you didn't ask for beer. Looks as if Ronnie took it all when he scarpered. Sit down.'

They each sat in an armchair. 'Were you and Ronnie married?'

She gave a sour grin. 'A bloke from the Willows? Do me a favour. They all *promise* to, once you're in a place of your own. Only problem is, they never seem to hang about that long.'

Crane gave her a sympathetic smile. She at least had those lavender eyes. Decent figure too. Small-breasted and slightly boyish, but it was the sort of figure that stayed where it was when the curvy ones were getting middle-aged and hefty. She sipped her drink.

'It cuts both ways. If they don't marry you they can't take anything when they do a runner. *I* bought this gear, on the weekly. All he had was that bloody car and I hope he's living in it.'

'How do you get to work? Bus?'

'No, I bought a Fiesta, on the drip, like the furniture. It's old but it goes. I could just about run to it once I didn't need to pay for everything, with Ronnie never managing to get his hand in his pocket. I put a lot of over-time in and I'll always work Sundays.' The fate of plain girls on the Willows seemed to be that if you could get a man at all he expected to be bought and paid for. Crane's mobile rang.

'Geoff here, Frank,' Anderson said breezily. 'Just wondered if you'd got any further since we saw Mahon?'

Crane swore silently. He supposed he'd better get used to this, hard as it was for a man like him. 'Oh hello, Geoff,' he said evenly. 'It could be I have made some kind of a breakthrough. I picked up on you asking Mahon where Cliff was. It struck me it might be worth talking to him. I asked Patsy Jackson if she could put me in touch. I'm at Patsy's place now.'

There was a brief silence. 'What ... made you think he could tell you anything? He was one of those—'

'Because of their bust up,' Crane cut him off. 'I wondered *why* there was a bust up. Well, it was because Greenwood also believed Mahon had seen off Donna.' Crane filled him in on the rest.

There was a longer silence. Then, 'Bugger!'

'Come again?'

'I should have seen that. But even if I had I'd never have thought Greenwood would grass him.'

'I got lucky. Patsy filled me in on his going straight. He'd had a bellyful of being in trouble with the law. It gave me a lever. I also promised him I'd keep his name out of anything.'

Another silence and then Anderson said, 'I knew you were good, Frank, but there was no need to rub my nose in it.'

He spoke lightly and Crane knew he'd be grinning, but he also knew that Anderson's professional pride had had a hole kicked through it. This gave him a small smile of his own. He'd got one over on the whiz kid who'd lived with the case since the body had left the water. At the same time, it had gone against all his own professional instincts

55

to let the information on Greenwood go. He just didn't work that way. Other people could be a distraction, especially a clever reporter who, according to Carol at the Glass-house, had a compulsion to take over and run things. But he had to keep reminding himself that Anderson's brain was stocked with information about the Donna Jackson affair that could take Crane many hours to assemble.

Anderson's grin was wiped away as he cleared his phone. How could he have slipped up on a detail like that? He'd been convinced he knew *everything* about everyone involved in Donna's killing. Why hadn't he checked out Greenwood himself? Why had he assumed that none of Mahon's mates would ever go straight? What else was Crane going to pick up on? He *had* to know, and know as it was happening, to be able to make that final award-winning feature absolutely authentic, apart from anything else. He wondered how he could get in closer with Crane. But then, why had a man who tended to be as close with information as he himself was, let go the details of Greenwood's confession? Because Crane was forcing himself into a quid pro quo for what *he* knew. It gave him an idea and his grin began to return.

'That was Geoff Anderson, Patsy. We're pooling information, as he knows so much about the case, possibly even more than the police. He was a bit miffed about me getting ahead of him, thanks to you.'

'He's a good looking bloke, that Geoff. They must be queuing up to loofah his back. What will you do now? About Bobby?'

He shrugged. 'I need to find a way of proving he wasn't at home that night, without involving Cliff. It won't be easy, but if I can I can hand it back to the police. If he wasn't at home he'll have to prove he wasn't with Donna, and if he is guilty I don't think he'll be able to, the state he's in just now.'

She sighed, her face in shadow, her hair back-lit in an untidy halo from one of the table lamps. 'Poor Bobby, he's been a silly beggar, but it does upset me to see him wandering round the Willows and everyone pretending he's the Invisible Man. He'd *never* have done that to her, not Bobby, not if she hadn't set out to upset him so badly he ...' The sentence dangled.

'He could be trying to convince himself he *hasn't* done it. Too much to cope with. I've known it happen. The mind's a funny thing.'

'He's nothing like as bad as they paint him. It's that crap home life. Fancy another drink?'

'No, thanks all the same. With the driving ...'

She nodded with a small fatalistic smile. Expecting nothing she was never going to be disappointed.

Crane put on his jacket, touched her arm. 'Thanks for everything, Patsy, you knowing Cliff was going straight swung it for me. I hope you'll go on helping me, if I need more information.'

She flushed again. 'I'll help any way I can. But all I really know is the Willows and the folk on it.'

'Exactly. No one knows the place like you do.'

When he'd gone, Patsy thought what a great bloke he was. Tall, tough, nothing in the way of looks, but his manner ... so polite. Opening car doors for you, praising you when you didn't think you'd done anything much. She knew he didn't like her hair, she could tell by the way he'd looked at it back at Mam's that first time. It had made her angry, really angry. But later she'd thought, well, at least he'd looked. Men on the Willows couldn't care less what she looked like, if they'd go out with her at all. All they were bothered about was getting her into bed, and they never seemed to think that was any big deal either. She gave herself another drink, looked at herself in a glass, wiped away a tear. If only she could get off with a bloke like Crane. If only she'd never had a sister like Donna ...

Crane drove back to his house on Bentham Terrace, put away his Renault. As he left the garage, someone pinioned him from behind. Then someone else jumped in front of him and punched him in the belly. The man holding him had a grasp like a straitjacket, and though Crane kicked backwards he couldn't locate either of his legs. The fist went into his belly again. Then again and again. Five or six times until his guts felt as if they'd burst into flames.

'Let it go, mister,' a soft hoarse voice whispered in his ear. 'Donna Jackson. Otherwise, next time we've finished you'll have the tooth fairy round. It'll take her five minutes to pick 'em all up.'

Then they were off, running on soft-soled shoes to some car they'd have parked two streets away. Crane would have run after them except that he could barely walk, let alone run. He limped painfully to the back door, let himself in, slid gingerly down on to the kitchen tiles. He sat for ten minutes until the raging fire in his insides had settled to a steady burn. Then he levered himself up. He'd lie in a hot bath, smooth something on to ease the pain. At least it hadn't been blows to the head, which could be very bad news, as he knew from his police days.

His mobile rang. 'Frank … Crane.'

'It's Ted. You all right? You sound funny.'

'I've just had a kicking. Some scrotes telling me to lay off the Jackson case.'

'Go on! How long ago was it? Want me to get a car round?'

'Don't bother, Ted. They'll be long gone.'

'Well, if you're sure.' He was silent for a short time. 'Thing is, you needn't have had it, the kicking. This Mahon. He walked in the station late afternoon. Admitted to topping her. Put his hand up to the lot.'

'It would have saved us such a lot of heartache if he'd owned up right at the start.' Connie wiped away tears. 'We couldn't begin to cope with it in the first place, our lovely girl ... but to have him swaggering round the Willows, giving out it had nothing to do with him ...'

'Oh, Mam.' Patsy put a hand on her arm. 'He didn't swagger, you know he didn't, not with folks turning their backs on him, pretending he wasn't there. He *knew* what a terrible thing he'd done, knew as well as we did. He couldn't have meant to do it.'

'Won't bring her back though!' Malc broke out, face crumpled in grief. 'Whether he meant it or not. I'd see the bugger hang. It's only a pity they ever done away with it. He'll be out in his thirties, they don't even serve a proper sentence these days. I'd see the bugger hang.' He put hands over his face and began to sob.

'Malc, love, don't take on ...'

Crane could detect both sadness and exasperation in Patsy's glance. She'd have to go through it all again and she'd already had too much, even though she'd loved Donna too – when she wasn't bitterly envying her her glamour.

'We don't know how to thank you, Frank,' Connie said in a tremulous tone. 'I can't think what you did.'

'Not a lot, Connie, to be honest,' Crane said, putting a hand over hers. 'He was in a state when Geoff and I talked to him. We could see it was all beginning to get on top of him, the way people on the Willows were treating him. And then Geoff telling him you'd set me on to make a fresh start and that I didn't give in too easily ...'

Silence fell again, one of the many during the past emotional half-hour. Crane couldn't get it together, couldn't quite believe it. The Mahons were a criminal family. They didn't do guilty pleas. If you were up for a crime, any crime, murder included, and you got away with it that was an end of the matter. You'd won.

But that powerful image Anderson had conjured up. The community of the Willows pointing the bone. It could be that the reporter had swung it. How much longer could Mahon have stood it before he'd had to slink away? And how would he survive away from the society that was all he'd ever known? He'd have ended up living rough, the English equivalent of an Aborigine taking himself wretchedly off to die alone in the outback. Prison must have seemed the better option.

'He'll know he's born if they bang him up in Armley!' Malc broke out again, ending the silence. 'If you're in for thieving join the club, but killing an innocent little kid like Donna ...'

'Leave it now, love,' Connie said quietly. As Crane got up to go, she jumped to her feet, put her arms round him and kissed him on the cheek. 'We all thank you, Frank, from the bottom of our hearts.'

They went with him into the narrow hall. 'Would you

drop me at the Conway, Frank?' Patsy asked. 'I walked over tonight.'

He nodded, waved goodbye to Connie and Malc, people he'd probably never see again, as with so many of the people he'd known briefly as they went through their bad times. But he'd not forget them.

'I like your new hairdo,' he told her, as he saw her into the car.

She flushed, shrugged, feigned indifference. 'Just thought I'd try something new.'

It fell in a straight simple style. The tousled look had emphasized the plainness of her features, but the new look had given them depth. She made Crane think of those actresses destined from girlhood to play mature parts, and who would only really come into their own in their thirties. As with luck, she might.

'The supervisor likes it, but the girls think it doesn't suit me,' she said uneasily.

'Probably just jealous,' he said, drawing up outside Conway House.

'You'll be too busy to come in for a drink,' she said flatly. There was no hope in her voice. Crane had gone back once. Plain girls from the Willows learnt very early not to get carried away.

'I'd like a drink.'

She gave him one of her confused glances. It renewed his sense of guilt. She'd had it right, he *was* too busy to go for a drink. The case was over, and so was her usefulness. Except for the one thing he still needed help with. He wondered why she'd suddenly had this costly new hairdo. It was almost as if she'd picked up on the bad vibes he'd had for the bird's nest it had been before. She'd also toned down the mask of make-up as if realizing it didn't go with the hair. Odd. She knew he'd want a G and T. When they were sitting down he couldn't stifle a groan of pain.

'Whatever's the matter?'

'When I got home last night, someone belted me in the guts.'

She gasped in shock, eyes widening.

'There were two of them. Hoodies. There was something funny about it. The one who gave me the knuckles, I think it could have been a woman. I got a smell of scent. If it *was* a woman she was tough, but if the bloke holding me had been doing the punching I'd have been in A and E.'

'What ... did it smell like?'

'Strong. Sort of spicy.'

'It could have been Myrtle Mahon,' she said slowly. 'She goes in for the heavy perfumes. Hefty too, knows how to take care of herself. A punter once tried to short-change her and she *did* put him in A and E.'

'The bloke said I had to lay off Donna's case. Well-built, about your height. Too big to be Dougie, as I remember him.'

'You're right. Dougie's small, wiry. Never gets involved in the kickings himself. Has minders for that.'

'Any idea who it could be then?'

She watched him in a long rueful silence, then sighed heavily. 'It was probably Marvin.'

'Your ... brother?'

'As if Mam and Dad hadn't enough on their plate. When I heard the whispers about Dougie and those fancy guns I just *knew* Marvin would be involved. He once worked for a security firm, servicing intruder alarms. He knows how to fix them so they don't go off and ring through to the bobbies. He's always been in with Dougie. What will you do?'

He watched her for a few seconds. He'd once been police and his every instinct was to get Marvin's collar felt. He said, 'I'm going to forget it, Patsy, if it's your brother. I just wondered what their game was, duffing me up like that. I reckon I know now.'

'Don't worry about him on my account,' she said brusquely. 'If he had to go inside again I honestly think he'd pack it in, the knock-off. He'd have a better living going straight, they all would.' She fell silent for a time, then added, with reluctance, 'I don't like saying this, and I've only ever said it to you, but I think it was a weight off his mind when Donna went in the reservoir.' Crane watched her again and waited. She said, 'I can't be sure, but I think Donna might have been leaning on him. He could make decent money now and then. He'd drive for Dougie, fix the alarms. He was a key bloke, really. I think Donna could find out what he was up to from Bobby. I'd not put it past her to have wheedled money out of him so she'd not spread it about. She always used the poor bugger. Effie hated her.'

'Effie?'

'Marvin's live-in.'

'Donna wasn't really very nice, was she?'

She sighed again. 'You needed to know her. She could twist people round her little finger. Not just blokes. She always looked such an innocent kid, as if she didn't know the way to the end of the street. She could get you to do things for her and make it seem she was doing *you* a favour.'

'I know the type well.' He got to his feet, wincing.

'Are you badly bruised? I've got some arnica, it's really, really good for bruising. I'll get it.'

'That's very thoughtful, Patsy.'

When he'd gone she sat over another drink, thinking about him and what a lovely bloke he was. Tough, not complaining about his injuries though he must still have been in pain. So good with Mam and Dad. Never saying anything he didn't mean. But he liked her new hairdo, so that *must* mean he'd disliked the way she'd had it before. There was something about Frank Crane that made you feel good. He just needed to be around. He hardly ever smiled, but when he did ...

Benson stood at the bar. The second Crane joined him he said, 'Look, Frank, this Bobby Mahon carry-on, it's solved nothing, it's just made things a bloody sight worse.'

Crane watched him, absently handing the barman a note.

'The silly sod comes down the nick, right, tears running down his face, says yes, it was him throttled her. So we dig out the file, get the tape going, tell him to get on with it.' He stabbed out his cigarette, felt for another. 'And we begin to find that nothing adds up, not one detail. Christ, we've got the SOC diagrams and measurements in front of us, we know the exact spot her body was fished out, the things she was wearing, how the bag of stones was attached, all of that. And nothing he told us, nothing at all, tallied with the facts.'

He inhaled smoke deeply. 'What a bloody *mess*. He just kept saying, "I done it, I done it, what more do you *want?*" and weeping and sobbing, but he couldn't tell it like it was. We rushed the bugger up to Tanglewood, said show us exactly where you dumped her, but he couldn't. He was nearly off his head by then. "Just charge me," he kept shouting. "Charge me and have done with it." But he got it wrong by twenty yards.'

Crane stood in stunned silence. Finally he said, 'Maybe he just forgot the exact place. It's been a year, after all.'

'Agreed. So we took him to the sluice-way end. That's where the stones came from, the buttressing. Hadn't a *clue* where they'd been gathered.'

'He ... could have forgotten that too. He struck me as a bloke who'd have trouble remembering what he did yesterday.'

He nodded wearily. 'We took all of that into account. So then we talked about the body. And when he wasn't weeping and wailing he couldn't get any of that right either. Hadn't a clue where he was supposed to have attached the bag of stones. Said he'd tied it to her ankles with rope.' He stared at Crane irritably. 'It was attached to her waist with a plastic-covered clothes line. Said the stones were in a black plastic bin bag; we've got the bloody things stored in the chamber of horrors and they're in a clear plastic sack. He said she was in jeans and a short jacket. Well, she was in a floral summer *dress.*'

Crane stood again in baffled silence. 'He no more killed the kid than I did, Frank,' Benson said finally.

Crane knew he was right. The police had to have proof. They had to have the same proof for an innocent man who said he was guilty as for a guilty man who said he was innocent.

'Crazy sod,' Benson said. 'Crazy *sod*! If he'd given us this crap last year we'd have had the bugger out of the mowing and kept at it. With him sticking to that fucking alibi we could never see it being anyone else.'

He stood flushed and angry. He'd be thinking of all the wasted hours, the overtime, the cancelled leave. Crane thought about the meeting at the Goose and Guinea, Anderson's kindly words about Aborigines. 'It could be a lot to do with the Willows pointing the bone, Ted.' He told him about the meeting. 'He was in a state. He'd had months of being given the elbow. Apart from that I think he was genuinely crazy about her. And then Geoff starts giving him the needle. I think he must have decided he'd have an easier life inside. Saying he'd done it and taking the porridge. At least he'd get his self-respect back. Sounds crazy but I can't think why else he'd do it.'

'Stupid arsehole! He still wouldn't tell us where he really was the night she went missing. He certainly wasn't at home with Dougie and that lot.'

'You're right. But he had to pretend he was. He was actually alibiing Dougie.'

'What's that supposed to mean?'

'You didn't hear this. The bloke who told me was Cliff Greenwood, Bobby's one-time best mate. He's a decent lad, going straight now. The night Donna fell in the pond Dougie was taking delivery of a van-load of expensive antique guns. The big house Morton way, yes?'

'Come again.' It was Benson's turn to look stunned.

'Did none of you tie Dougie to it? It had his dabs on, according to Greenwood.'

'We think Dougie Mahon's involved in *everything* to do with posh gear. Like Greenwood says, it had his dabs on. The guns were the sort of clean, careful job he sets up. But we had no proof, we never do with that bugger, and the burglary didn't come to light till a week later with the owner being away. By that time it was a back-burner job anyway, it was all Donna Jackson then.'

'Well, Dougie made doubly sure he was fire proof. Told Bobby and his mates to say everyone was at the Mahons' place that night. That's why Bobby daren't admit where he really was himself. Until now. There's a good chance he was clubbing in Leeds with some French totty called Nicole. If you want to have another go with the guns you could try putting the arm on Marvin Jackson. He's going to find it hard to prove he wasn't disabling intruder alarms at a big moorland house that night.'

'We'll get him in, those guns were worth a fortune. If we can tie him to the house we can tie him to Dougie.'

'If Marvin wasn't out thieving he could be in another kind of serious shit, now Bobby looks to be off the hook. I'll get back to you on that. It was certainly him who duffed me up. Him and Dougie's wife.'

Benson glanced at him. 'You OK now? She's given out the muscle before on Dougie's behalf, him being nine stone wet through. Christ knows why blokes want to give *her* one, must be like humping a rhino.'

Crane said, 'What happens now, about Donna?'

'Terry wants to re-assemble the team who worked on it the first time round. It'll take time, but so what, we've lost months already with that dozy bastard. I've got to go, Frank. Keep in touch.'

Crane watched him move off. No word of thanks for handing him valuable information that could see the guns recovered, brownie points to Benson. But then he'd not expected any thanks. Benson owed him for a lot more than information. He owed him for a debt he could never repay and debts of that size killed friendship. And Benson had once been his closest friend.

As Crane walked across the marble tiling of the reception area, the dark-haired girl called Carol was collecting a package from the desk. 'Frank, hi,' she said. 'I suppose you've come looking for Doctor Watson, though I suspect he sees himself more as Sherlock himself.'

He grinned. 'Is he about? If not I'll catch him later.'

'Yes he is, and I was hoping I might just talk him into taking me out tonight. So you've got to be seriously bad news, turning up like this.'

'I take it you and Geoff are an item?'

'I thought we were, but since he got his teeth into the DJ story it's not been the same.' She tossed her curly hair. 'I suppose you've got to admire the big dope,' she said, with rueful fondness, 'the way he clings on with it. He'll not forgive you, you know, if you sort it all out before he does. I *know* him. I'll tell him you're here.'

She went off before he could tell her the case would soon be back with the police and her chance of a night out with Anderson looked good.

'Frank!' Anderson walked rapidly across reception. Everything he did was rapid. Crane was sorry about the case being over as far as he was concerned, but relieved not to have to go on uneasily cooperating with a bumptious reporter.

'Geoff, it's good news, bad news, depending which way you look at it. Mahon. He's confessed to killing Donna, but the police aren't buying it.'

Anderson's mobile face became totally still, and when Crane had given him the story he watched him in a lengthy silence, and that was unusual too in a man who thought and talked so fast. The news had clearly given him a big shock, just as it had Crane. He finally gave a wry smile. 'You don't think this could be Mahon-type cunning? He puts his hand up and then deliberately gives all the wrong answers, so they have to let him go? He's cleared his name and he's off the hook for good.'

Crane shook his head. 'He's not got that kind of brain, we both know it. And with skilled CID men knowing all the ways to flush out the truth ... they're as certain now it wasn't Mahon as they were once certain it was. My feeling is he just couldn't go on facing any more of that shit the Willows was throwing at him. Benson says he was in a state of near-hysteria.'

'Christ,' he said softly. 'I was damn certain it was him, just like the police and the Willows, and one day I was sure someone would nail the bugger. I had that big write-up all there in my mind, you know, boy meets girl, all that stuff. Then girl begins to outclass boy. She's very popular and it's obvious she's going to make it as a model, probably a very good one. Boy can't hack it. He gets red-jealous, starts knocking her about, finally does her in; if he can't have her no one can. All set against the slagheap the Willows is these days. It's a classic.'

Crane watched him. It had to be the born journalist's mind in action. It *was* a classic, only there were real flesh and blood people involved: a dead beautiful kid, parents who endlessly grieved, a boyfriend off his trolley, a sister who'd had to handle most of the fallout despite having problems of her own.

Anderson shrugged. 'I shouldn't imagine Mahon's heard of Karl Popper's law of unintended consequences.

He puts his hand up to a killing everyone's desperate to get off the books and no one'll let him go near a slammer.'

Crane was to remember about Karl Popper and his ironic law very forcibly not long after.

FIVE

The second he opened the door Crane pushed him firmly backwards into the hall, stepped inside himself, then closed the door behind him.

'Hey, what's *your* game!' There was a savage glint in his eyes and his fists were clenched.

'I wouldn't, Marvin,' Crane said calmly. 'There's just you and me today, not you, me and Myrtle.'

That stopped him. Then he gave a sneery smile. 'No flies on you is there? I hope you don't think it's payback time. For your sake.'

'I'm not looking for trouble, Marvin, but I should warn you I don't smoke, don't drink a lot, and work out on a regular basis.'

'Either go now, pal, or get thrown through the door.'

'I'd do yourself a big favour and chill out, if I were you.'

But the other took a swing at him, which Crane was ready for and avoided. He then gave Jackson his right fist into the belly. It was a soft belly, with all the pints the man saw off, and air left his lungs like a burst tyre. He fell to his knees, cursing and groaning and clutching himself. It looked as if he should have done himself a favour and chilled out.

72

'What was that you were saying about the tooth fairy, Marvin?'

Crane saw the woman then, standing at the kitchen door at the end of the hall. She was small and spare and had sharp, close set features. She wore a grubby yellow T-shirt and drawstring shorts. Her reddish hair was in rollers. She looked as if she'd seen it all before. 'You silly sod!' she cried, in a piercing voice. 'Who do you owe money to *now*?'

Still clutching himself, Jackson muttered through clenched teeth, 'All right, so it was payback time. Now piss off, will you.'

'I told you I wasn't looking for trouble. I'm here to ask you a couple of questions.'

'Hey, mister, who the hell are you, anyway?'

'Shut it, Effie.'

'Don't tell *me* to shut it, you big dozy sod.'

'Just where were you the night your sister died, Marvin?'

He looked at Crane uneasily through slate-blue eyes. He had the plain Jackson features, not helped by the shaved head. 'What's it to you?' he said, as he got wincing to his feet.

'A lot, take my word.'

'How would I know? It must be a year.'

'Everyone on the Willows knew what they were doing when they found out Donna hadn't come home, she was so well-known. It's a bit like the Sunday morning we heard the news about Princess Di, isn't it? It kind of sticks in the mind, And you were Donna's brother.'

'Don't say you're digging all the crap up again,' Effie cried. 'Not that trollop—'

'Effie, will you for fuck's sake keep your neb out?'

'Nothing but trouble. Well, tell him, nothing but trouble and aggravation, that one, day she was born.'

'You know they've had Bobby Mahon down at the nick, don't you? There's not much you miss on the Willows. Well, did you know they're certain to release him, because they don't believe he did it, even though he says he did.'

He hadn't heard. He watched Crane in a puzzled silence. 'So?'

'So that's why I need to know where *you* were that night.'

'Here, you're not making out it were anything to do with me?'

'She was into you for money, wasn't she, for some reason?'

'Who told you that?'

'I get paid to find things out.'

'Into him for money!' Effie screeched. 'The little twat was never off his back: twenty here, twenty there, then there's not enough to pay the sodding rent book.'

'I'm warning you, Effie—'

'I was *glad*! I was glad some bugger threw her in the frigging reservoir. Couldn't see why he'd left it so long.'

'One more word—'

'Go on, you daft clown, you fancied her yourself. Think I'm blind? I know you think I'm stupid.' Her shrill, cawing tones were suddenly raw with a distilled bitterness. Her voice resounded in the silence. Jackson had reddened, his eyes fell from Crane's.

'Is that what she put the bite on you far?' Crane said, in a voice too soft for Effie to catch. 'Did something happen between you and Donna when she was under age and you were over? Something she wanted hush money for? Something Malc would have put you in A and E about, if not a coffin?'

Jackson still couldn't meet his eyes. 'She didn't need no encouragement,' he muttered. 'Fourteen or not.'

'What's going on?' Effie scuttled along the hall. 'What you whispering about? I'm supposed to be your partner.'

'I was just telling him what's likely to happen if he doesn't get his story right about where he was the night Donna died,' Crane told her. 'Because now Bobby's out of the frame they're going to take a closer look at all her other contacts' – he gave each of them in turn a hard stare – 'who might have been glad to see Donna out of it for one reason or another.'

Her pinched features were now as flushed as Jackson's beneath the line of rollers. 'He was with me, mister,' she said hurriedly. 'As true as God's my judge.'

'I don't believe you, Effie. It was the antique guns, Marvin, yes, Dougie's big one? You want my advice, you'll put your hand up to that or they're going to go after you for Donna's killing. They'll dig it all up, about her being into you for money and ... all the rest. I reckon you've got two choices.'

'Oh, shit!' Effie wailed. 'He's trying to go straight, for fuck's sake. He's already been inside.'

'I know, Effie, but there's one job he's not paid for.'

He left them standing in the hall in a numbed and wretched silence.

Crane's mobile rang. 'Frank Crane.'

'Ted here, Frank. Mahon's completely cleared. We knew he would be, but we told the silly sod that if he'd really cared about Donna it'd help us to find the real killer if he told us the truth. Well, he really had been in Leeds with the French totty. He finally came up with a postcard he'd got from her. She'd written from Fontainebleu with a full address. It's dated four days after the Saturday in question and actually refers to the clubbing *last* Saturday and him being most of the night with her. He must have given her a belt round the chops so she'd not forget him ...'

Once again he sat with the Jacksons in their cramped living room. Once again emotion seemed to thicken the air. 'Dear God,' Malc muttered, hunched in his chair and staring into space, features expressionless. 'We were positive it were him, every last one of us.'

'These things sometimes happen, Malc,' Crane told him. 'I'm very sorry. It means starting from scratch, I'm afraid. The police are aiming to re-assemble the original team who worked on it. I think we can safely leave it to them now.'

'No, carry on, Frank,' Connie said, in a sad, firm voice. 'You got things going, when no one else did, even if it only showed it wasn't Bobby.'

'I'd like to stay with it, Connie, but you need to think about the cost.'

'It doesn't matter, the money. We'd not have another day's peace of mind if we didn't think we'd done everything we could. We owe it to our darling daughter, God rest her.' The skin around her eyes seemed permanently roughened and red with the endless weeping of the last twelve months.

'You go right ahead, Frank,' Malc said in a wavering tone, dabbing his own eyes with a handkerchief. 'It's what we both want.'

Crane glanced at Patsy. She was as impassive as before, unable to dredge up any more emotion for her dead sister, even though she'd loved her too, with a love Crane felt was maybe surer than theirs, based as it was on her wry acceptance of what she'd known the real Donna to be like.

He got up. 'All right, I'll give it my best shot. I'll be in touch. Need a lift, Patsy?'

'Please.'

Connie and Malc saw them out as usual, standing in the light of the small lamp above the front door, Malc's arm protectively about Connie's bowed form. Crane had seen much human misery in his time with the force but had never been able to handle it as professionally as he should. He thought, 'Christ, I'll nail the bastard if it's the last thing I do.' He wasn't to know that it very nearly was.

Anderson was holding centre stage again at the Glasshouse. 'That's right,' he was saying, 'and if a Chinese kid wants to learn the piano they get him going on a simple piece called "Knives and Forks".'

He had the others laughing, but Carol knew he was in a mood. It was almost impossible to spot unless you knew him well. There'd be that faintly abstract look in his eyes, the slightest impression that he wasn't giving his full attention to being the life and soul of the party, although his brain spun at such a speed that he was always able to deal with any number of conflicting thoughts at the same time.

'You want to come back to my place for a bite, Carol?' he said, when the others were talking generally.

'You're not working tonight?'

'I should be, but all work and no play ...'

Yet Carol knew he never played, not these days, and though he'd be jolly and chatty back at his flat, she'd know in the occasional silences that he was brooding about the Donna Jackson business, brooding with a new intensity now that Bobby Mahon had been cleared.

'We'll have one more before we go then.' And he was off to the bar, though not bouncing with his usual restless energy.

Carol knew that Mahon being out of it had messed up that big feature he'd wanted to write, that he was positive would help him in his ambition to be an investigative journalist on a paper like *The Sunday Times*. There'd be another ending to the Donna killing and he'd dig it all out brilliantly, but they both knew it wasn't going to have the same impact. Frank Crane was bugging him too, though she knew he also reluctantly admired him, the way he could ferret things out that Geoff was kicking himself that *he'd* not picked up on. He was so competitive, forever wanting to spot the bad lots before the police did. He'd be impossible to live with if Crane got ahead of him now, after all the work he'd put in, though Crane was probably off the case with the police reopening their files. She wished to God Geoff was. It had been nothing but Donna Jackson since they'd pulled the poor kid out of Tanglewood. She sighed. A flesh and blood rival she could cope with, but a dead beauty? Yet she couldn't help loving the big dope. Things would be different when he made it to London. Then that provoked another dismal thought: would he take her with him?

At the bar, Anderson could brood in peace, not feeling he had to be the amiable charmer he'd spent his working life perfecting. He just couldn't get Mahon's innocence out of his head. It messed everything up, every bloody thing. Donna and that piece of rubbish had been the story. The way he'd decided to write the big feature was carefully to imply that it couldn't have been anyone else but Mahon, let the reader draw his own conclusions. And then Mahon was suddenly out of the frame. What was the story going to be now? Would it have anything like the same force? He doubted it. He switched on a cheery smile for the bar girl who brought his drinks, who he knew fancied him. Well, at least it must mean that clever sod Crane was off the case, he could do without him turning up the leads that should have been his. That break Crane had had with Cliff Greenwood still stung.

He sat down with Carol, faithful Carol, whose body had stopped turning him on some time ago, though her clever, well-read mind was still a big draw, and the tasty meals she cooked for him. It would be all over when he went to London. Alone, definitely alone. London would solve everything.

Patsy could hardly believe it, but Frank was in her little flat a third time! It couldn't be the new hairstyle, could it, and the care she was taking with her clothes and make-up? She went off to get the drinks, leaving Crane with a renewed sense of guilt. He had an idea the kid was getting a little struck on him, when the only reason he was back here again was the original one – her knowledge of the Willows and the people Donna had mixed with. He'd need her help and also the help of that brash, talented prat, Anderson.

When she came back with the drinks, she said, 'Where will you go from here, Frank?'

'Talk it over with Geoff first. He said he'd always be willing to help. It's in his own interests, of course, wanting to break a story he's spent so much time on.'

'He's a nice bloke. He was very kind with Mam and Dad.'

'I'll try and pin him down this evening, though I daresay he'll be on some job or other. People like me and him don't do time off.'

'You ... could ask him to come here, if you like. I might be able to help.'

'You know, Patsy, that's a very good idea,' Crane said, and meant it. 'You had the inside track on Donna, if anyone.'

'I don't think anyone had the real inside track on that little madam.' But she looked very pleased he'd taken the suggestion seriously. Crane began to key Anderson's number.

'Geoff Anderson.'

'Frank Crane, Geoff. Look, Connie and Malc want me to stay on the case. It shouldn't affect the new police investigation, it'll probably take them a week to get people off other things and back on to this. I'm at Patsy's place. I wondered if you could find a little time to spend with us and talk the thing through?'

'Give me half an hour, Frank.'

Anderson snapped shut his mobile. 'Look, Carol, something's come up. Sorry about the evening. Another time, eh?'

'Donna Jackson,' she said dejectedly. She was more than used to seeing him rushing off when there'd been a drugs bust or a knifing, but the DJ story was so *old*. Why couldn't

Crane see Geoff in the morning, when he usually did have some spare time?

'Crane's like a pig with a truffle, Carol. He's wasted time and the Jacksons' money by this Mahon nonsense.' He gave her a quick kiss. 'Next free night, I *promise* ...'

And then he was bounding off, more his old eager self than he'd been ever since he'd learnt about Mahon. She wished she didn't love him quite so much. She was almost certain, if he got to London, she'd not see him again.

'What sort of day have you had?' Crane asked her, as they waited for Anderson over the drinks.

'The sort of day I always have. I'm a checkout, remember?'

'But you must be in line for some kind of promotion after all this time.'

She coloured in that way she had. 'Oh, I don't want a promotion. I'm happy with the girls. If I took a step up I'd be over them and it wouldn't be the same.'

Crane thought, poor kid, she had so little confidence, seemed so defenceless against peer pressure, not just among the sort of women who lived on the Willows, but among her mates on the tills.

'Funny you should mention it though, because my supervisor said did I want to think about moving up a peg.'

That would have been when she'd ditched the tousled hair and the layers of make-up, Crane guessed. 'Why not go for it, Patsy?'

'The other girls, they'd think ... they can be a bit catty.'

'You'd learn to live with it. And you'd get on, make more money. You always felt Donna had all the attention and you lost out. Well, now's the time to make up for it.'

'Oh, I don't know, Frank.'

'Just *go* for it. If they're wanting to promote you they must think you're the right type.'

Patsy had never known her confidence to be given such a boost. But then, she'd never known anyone like Frank. He never seemed to be flannelling, he just seemed to say exactly what he thought. And he must think there was *something* about her ...

Crane felt it was the least he could do, help her find herself after the years of living in her sister's shadow, of unsuitable men, mundane work. A quid pro quo for the help she'd already given him and that she would hopefully continue to give him. It would help to ease the slight persistent guilt a little.

Anderson came rushing in, holding a collapsible stand that already had a flipchart screwed to it.

Crane said, 'What's all this?'

'If we're brainstorming we might as well do this as methodically as possible.'

'What's wrong with using our memories, for Christ's sake?'

'If we write everything down here nothing gets overlooked. And Patsy's memory won't have had the training ours have had.'

'You can say that again, Geoff,' she said, but she was very pleased to be involved like this with two men who were so different from the sorts of men she was used to.

As usual, it went against all Crane's instincts, which were to work alone and keep his cards close. Yet he'd done exactly this type of thing in the police force, when information was coming in by the shed load, the felt tips on the white boards, noting everything that seemed crucial. But then, they'd all been police together, working to a common goal. Anderson had his own agenda, and if everything went on the flipchart he'd almost certainly feel more in control, no detail lost for the big feature he'd set his ambitions on, with Crane unable to get too far ahead of him. Crane wondered what it mattered if it got them anywhere? Except that his professional pride was coming into it now and he *wanted* to get there ahead of Anderson.

'Do you guys want a drink?'

They both nodded and Anderson said, 'I like your new hairstyle, Patsy, by the way. You've changed it haven't you since I used to visit your folks?'

'Glad you like it,' she said, going quickly off to the kitchen.

'She's different,' he said. 'Just used to sit there when I was talking to Connie and Malc. Hair a dog, make-up laid on with a trowel, tended to be sullen.'

'She did a good job for me with Greenwood and I told her so. I'm also encouraging her to go for promotion. She's not a bad kid, just lost her confidence with the spotlight always being on Donna.'

'Donna was a taker and she had a lot to answer for.' He turned back to the flip chart and wrote the word DONNA at the top of the first page in felt tip and underlined it. 'Right,' he said briskly. 'Let's jot down on this page everyone we know to have been in contact with her.'

'Maybe we should start with the kid who found her.'

He shrugged. 'If you like, but that's all he did, find the body. I tried to get a little story out of him but he was having nightmares and it was his father who gave me the outline and then told me to sod off, they'd all had more than enough with the police.' But he wrote down LIAM PATTERSON.

'Thanks, Patsy,' he said, taking his drink from the offered tray. 'Donna knew Clive Fletcher before Joe Hellewell, right?'

'She was barely out of school before Fletcher got his beady eye on her. God knows how he does it.' She gave a shudder. '*Cre-epy.*'

'He trawls the clubs,' he told her. 'I've seen him around.'

'The photographer,' Crane said, 'who may or may not have talked her into nude photography? You gave him a clean bill of health in your reports.'

'I had to watch my step. The readers know him as a weddings and babies man. It was only the insiders who knew the truth and they didn't talk.' His grin was faintly conspiratorial. There was plenty a skilled journalist could imply about a man like Fletcher, but Crane guessed it was to be the big story again, with Donna cast as the innocent she'd looked. Anderson said, 'I suggest we see the bloke as soon as we can.' He wrote down CLIVE FLETCHER on the chart and below that he wrote JOE HELLEWELL.

'*He* was a bit creepy too,' Patsy said. 'He was good looking and seemed all right, so I don't really know why. Only met him the once.'

'Agreed. Another arsehole and I couldn't get a fix on him either. Attractive wife. Gave an impression she was making do. We'll see him as well. Pity about the rock hard alibi.'

Crane knew this was going to be the problem. The case had been picked over in such detail he wondered if there could possibly be any area left he could shine his own little torch into that hadn't already been floodlit. He picked up the felt tip and scribbled MARVIN JACKSON and EFFIE.

'What's all this?' Anderson said. 'Patsy's *brother?*'

'Donna was definitely putting the squeeze on Marvin for some hold she had over him,' Crane said. He wasn't going to spell it out, not in front of Patsy.

'How do you know this?'

'Patsy tipped me off and I went to see him.'

'Now come on, you bugger, I thought we'd agreed to act together.' He spoke lightly and with his usual disarming grin, but Crane could sense the underlying irritation. He was beginning to realize just how much of a control freak Anderson really was and how driven to try and take over. And this was the second time Crane had come up with an extra angle on a case he'd lived and breathed. The reporter gave Patsy a slight look of reproach. It was clear he felt it was him she should have tipped off.

She reddened. 'I told no one at the time, Geoff. It wasn't just because he was my brother, it was because I had a bloody good idea ...'

She broke off, embarrassed. Crane said, 'What Patsy's saying is that Marvin probably had the best alibi of all. We think the police believe he was involved in an unrelated matter that night.'

Anderson didn't like that either, even if you could barely tell, but Crane didn't want him rushing into print about anything to do with antique guns until Benson was good and ready.

'All right, you cagey sod,' Anderson said, in the amused tone he'd perfected, 'but I've got my own snouts at the station.'

'Fair enough,' Crane said. 'Anyway Marvin's live-in's another matter. Effie. She detested Donna. Whether she detested her enough to kill her and had the nous is highly unlikely but not impossible. Let's regard her as a long shot.'

Anderson turned back to the flip chart and began to write each name listed on the front sheet on to a separate sheet of its own. His edgy movements told Crane that behind the collected exterior he was still very annoyed. 'Now,' he said, 'can we think of anyone else she knew who might have a possible motive? Anyone at all. Patsy?'

'That was the trouble, she knew so many people, mainly blokes. And she was so secretive. She got off on it. She'd only ever hint at things. "I'm going for a Chinese with this guy who has a look of Brad Pitt. If Bobby comes round tell him I'm at Auntie Linda's." All that stuff.'

'OK. Now, on these separate sheets let's think about motivation. Take Fletcher. Maybe Donna got to know too much about his operation but refused to get involved herself?' He jotted down KNEW TOO MUCH?

Crane said, 'Blackmail?' Anderson wrote that down too.

'He might have lost it with her because she'd not have sex with him,' Patsy said. 'She led blokes on, even when there was no way she was going to sleep with them.'

He scribbled down CRIME OF PASSION?

They did the same for the others, working through possible motives. Crane had to grudgingly admit that it did help focus their minds, especially Patsy's, and time passed quickly.

'Well, that makes a start, you guys,' Anderson said, flicking his thick mop of wavy hair back and finishing his drink. 'Every time we get back here we jot down everything we've turned up. Oh, is it OK to use your pad, Patsy?'

She nodded quickly, touchingly eager to be of use.

'I'll be off then. But you will keep me on message, Frank?'

'The problem's solved, isn't it,' Crane said, with an ironic smile of his own, 'now you've got the flip chart up and running?'

'I'm a reporter and we do like to be where it's at when anything's actually happening.'

It was a fair point, Crane supposed, but it emphasized again the separate directions they were coming from, the newspaperman anxious for all the publicity and headlines he could grab, and the PI, keen to keep his work and himself as low profile as possible. He'd always sensed that taking the chance of working with him was going to be a two-edged sword.

The atmosphere seemed flat when Anderson had gone as when he was around you could almost feel the energy he seemed to throw off like blown air.

'Another drink, Frank?'

'A very small one,' he said, telling himself to bring a little stock of booze with him next time, the kid had little enough spare cash. He flicked through the sheets of the flip chart. Could it be one of them, he wondered, or one of those secret punters who might never now be traced, however hard they brainstormed? He sighed.

'Thanks.' He took the fresh drink she handed him. She seemed to be mutating before his eyes. It wasn't just the hair and the make-up she was looking to, but also her clothes. She wore a crisp white square-neck top, lilac, narrow leg trousers and newish black mules. He sat with her on the sofa. It was obvious she'd loved working with them this evening.

'Patsy, when the police searched Donna's room after she'd gone missing they'd have been hoping to find letters, a diary. Especially a diary.'

She nodded. 'That's what Mr Benson said. We were there while they went through her things. They found nothing like that and they looked everywhere, even under the mattress. Her bed has drawers in the base, they took every single thing out.'

'Did they look under the carpet?'

She shook her head. 'It's fitted. You can't move it.'

'There could just be a little part that's loose. My granny used to keep a few tenners in an envelope in a place like that.'

'I could take another look.'

'Might be worth a try. Has anything been done with the place since?'

She shook her head, gave a slight grimace. 'They've kept it exactly as it was. Like a … what's the word?'

'Shrine?'

She nodded. 'I'll have a scout round next time I'm there.'

'Good girl.'

He got ready to go. He patted her arm, gave her a warm smile. She was searching for her own self-worth as hard as he was searching for Donna's killer. And it seemed that Donna had had to die for the complex chain reaction to be triggered which could lead to Patsy being given a chance to live.

Later, Patsy couldn't sleep for thinking about him. Three times he'd been here and would be here more, with

Geoff, the men *listening* to what she had to say, so keen to use what little she knew. She'd never known anything like it. She wondered, could Crane be, could he possibly be, interested in her? She knew she wasn't much of a looker, but neither was he, but what a bloke! He really seemed to like coming here, having a drink with her, and she didn't think he was living with anyone, at least that was the feeling she had. Life had never seemed like it was now, and it was just since she'd met Frank.

Crane blended in with the women and scattering of men who waited to pick up their children. As Liam Patterson only lived a couple of roads away, and it was summer, Crane hoped he took himself home. The boy came drifting across the playground with two others. 'Liam? Liam Patterson? Could I have a word with you?'

He eyed Crane suspiciously. He was small but chunky, with spiky brown hair, a pink, downy face and a snub nose. 'You think I'm getting in that car, pal, you're out of your tree,' he said in a piping voice. 'We don't go nowhere with strangers.'

Crane put on a friendly smile. 'I'm not asking you to, Liam. I'm helping the police. About the lady in the reservoir.'

'Not *that* again. Haven't they nobbled anyone? The fuzz are rubbish.'

'Couldn't catch a fish in a bucket!'

'Couldn't catch a burglar with a wooden leg!'

'Couldn't catch a torcher with his pants on fire!' The list of police inadequacy went on for some time. Crane waited patiently. At least the three seemed in no hurry to move on.

'When you used to swim in the reservoir, how late would you stay?'

'Listen, we need to split, mister—'

'Ninety-nines all round if you answer a couple of questions.' Glancing cautiously about him, Crane showed them the edge of a fiver.

'You don't want no change?'

'It's yours.'

'You couldn't make it a tenner?'

'No.'

'OK, man, a couple of questions.'

'Swimming in the reservoir, how late would you stay?'

'Till it started getting dusky. Till the funny men started hanging about, up on the other reservoir.'

'Funny men?'

'Queers,' he said.

'Poofters,' said another.

'Arse bandits,' said the third.

They began to giggle.

'Did any of these men talk to you boys?'

'Only Ollie.'

'Ollie?'

'Ollie Stringer. He's always around. He'd watch us swimming. Didn't try nothing on though. Daren't. We'd have had the Bill on him, no bother.'

'The police have *some* uses then?' But the blank stares reminded Crane that youngsters didn't usually do irony. 'What does he look like, this Ollie?'

'Fat. Has glasses with no edges. Always wears a straw hat.'

'Look … Liam, you went home when the light started going, but did you ever see the lady called Donna at Tanglewood with anyone when she was still alive?'

'You said two questions, mister. This is about ten.'

'That's the last one,' Crane said, giving the knowing urchin another warm smile. 'Can you remember someone as pretty as the lady was with a bloke around there?'

'Nah, she was just dead meat to me, buddy.'

Crane wondered which forbidden shocker he'd been watching, *Goodfellas* or *Reservoir Dogs*? But then the boy's downy face became impassive in the afternoon sun and he wondered how many frightful, recurrent dreams he'd had about trawling the bottom of a murky sheet of water and getting hold of a handful of pale dead flesh.

'Frank Crane.'

'It's Terry Jones, Frank. How are you doing?'

'Nice to hear from you, Terry.' It was too, DI Terry Jones had once been Crane's boss when he'd been in the force.

'Marvin Jackson. Ted tells me it's time for some collar-feeling.'

'I'm certain he'll admit to the fancy guns. Otherwise he knows he'll be a suspect for Donna's death. She was definitely into him for money.'

He gave Jones the details of what had happened between Jackson and his sister. 'He's scared shitless about any of that coming out. He knows he's just got the one option.'

'Bloody good effort, Frank. I've been in touch with Leicester, that's where the guns were sold in a district auction. A go-between put them in the sale, then the gang bought them back themselves, cash down. It only cost them a small commission and then they've got a bona fide bill of sale to show private buyers they're the legal owners.'

'Clever stuff.'

'No one can fix these things like Dougie. The police still haven't nabbed the gear but they know damn fine who's involved. If your friend Marvin coughs we'll be able to establish a link between Dougie and the gang, and we should be in business.'

'Glad I could help, Terry.'

'Tell me, are you still working on the Jackson case?'

'The Jacksons rehired me. I told them your people would be making a fresh start, but they'd not take no for an answer. I'll not get under your feet.'

'You never do. And as far as I'm concerned, the more brains involved in that particular can of worms the better. You must come for a bite of supper one night, Frank ...'

Jones put down his phone. Christ, he wished Crane were back. There'd been big trouble. Crane had fixed some evidence against one of the most evil types the city had ever known. Top class lawyers had picked up on it, Crane was out. Jones sighed, turned back to the file on the antique guns. It hadn't been just down to Crane, but also to Ted Benson, he was sure of it. He was sure too that Crane had taken the burn for the lot, as he was single and Benson had kids and a sick wife. That was the sort of bloke Crane was, apart from being the sharpest Jones had ever had on his team.

It had been a clear day and the setting sun was now a bright sliver through the dense trees of the low hills that surrounded the two sheets of water. Mallard, moorhens and Canada Geese clucked softly at the water's edge, their night quarters beneath overhanging foliage. Crane climbed the curving flight of wide stone steps that led from the lower to the upper reservoir. He spotted the straw hat almost instantly, on the head of a plump man in rimless glasses, who sat on a bench at the side of the perimeter track, gazing out over still water.

Crane sat on the same bench, about a yard from him. His faded blue eyes darted to Crane's through strong lenses. He had soft, pink, blobby features that gave an impression his face had no real bone structure. He wore a neatly ironed blue shirt and chinos. 'Looking for company, dear?' he said hopefully, in a high, slightly wheezing tone.

'Are you Ollie?'

He gave a little smile. 'Perhaps I should say, "Who's asking?" like they do on the telly.'

'Frank Crane.'

'It's a nice name and you've a nice friendly smile, but I don't believe I've seen it before, so it makes me just a tad wary.'

'Remember a young woman called Donna Jackson, Ollie?'

'Dear boy, if you're a bobby, despite that disarming cotton shirt and those form-fitting linen trousers, I shan't even admit to being called Ollie. I'm Bill Brown to the police, Frank Crane, always was.'

'I'm just a private investigator, working for Donna's parents.'

'Don't believe I like PI much either, dear, it's like saying you're not a crab but a lobster. They can both give you a very nasty nip.'

A twenty-pound note rustled between Crane's fingers.

'Oh!' Ollie gave a little coquettish scream. '*Specie.* I'm quite overwhelmed. It's usually the other way about, duckie, when you get to my age.'

'Look, Ollie, I know you don't talk to the police, you and your friends up here. I'm not wanting to intrude. I'm just an ordinary bloke working for two very distressed people whose daughter was strangled and dumped in the lower reservoir. Now it's not easy to get to Tanglewood without wheels unless you live nearby. I daresay you all have a fix on one another's motors, was there one you couldn't place roundabout the time she went missing?'

'You're dead wrong there, dear. *I* can't afford wheels on my bit of pension. Out through the door at fifty. "We're having to downsize, Ollie, I'm afraid," he says. "Oh," I say, "is it just gays you're downsizing, Mr Havercroft, because you only look to be downsizing by one?" Didn't know where to look, love, didn't know where to *put* himself. Terrified I'd go to the Tribunal. But I still got bleeding downsized.'

'But you know everyone, Ollie, don't you? I bet you're their first port of call for a good gossip.'

He liked that, almost simpered. 'Well, yes, they do like chewing the fat with their Auntie Ollie. That's what they call me. So very Gallic.' He took the note from Crane's fingers almost absently. 'Well, you have a trustworthy face. Now this is absolutely on the qui vive. We did see rather a lot of a young chap called Adrian along here, and the whisper was that he'd been seen getting out of a motor with your Donna and going off round the bottom reservoir.'

'The night she—'

'Oh, no.' He broke Crane off. 'It was a month or two before that.'

Crane was puzzled. ' But ... if he was one of your little group ...?'

'The word was he was a fiver each way, love.'

'Bisexual?'

'Never could get that carry-on together myself, but there you are.'

'And he's not been seen around any more? After that night?'

'Oh, yes, he was around a good while after the upset. But he just drifted off in the end, like they very often do. Probably got work outside the area. Couldn't say just when, I lose track of time at my age.'

'But it was definitely him, getting out of the car with Donna?'

'We're almost certain, love. But it was dusky and he was wearing a cap and wasn't in his usual car. That's why it's just a whisper, think on.'

'What did he look like? How old?'

'Fair, tallish, kept himself in nice shape. About forty.'

'And you're sure he was a fiver each way?'

'Well, sometimes he'd be around and sometimes not, and when he wasn't the word was he fancied the other side of the bed. And then there'd be those distasteful jokes flying around about the girlfriend being so confused she'd not know which way to turn.' He pursed his lips in disapproval.

'It's worth another twenty, Ollie, if you can find out where this Adrian went, and what his surname and occupation were, and what make of car he mostly used. Someone here must have the inside track.'

The idea seemed to excite him, maybe gave a little zest to what must have been an empty existence since Mr Havercroft had been forced to let him go. 'I'd not want my name coming into anything.'

'You have my word. I always protect my sources.'

He liked that too. He adjusted his Panama hat so the brim came a little lower over his eyes. 'All right, young man, I'll see what I can do. I must say you've got a very persuasive manner with you.'

'Good. I'll be back here, same time, same bench, the evening after next, yes?'

Ollie touched his arm. 'Are you quite sure you're straight, dear?'

Crane grinned again. 'Straight as a stick, Ollie. Awfully sorry I can't oblige.'

The three of them stood in Patsy's living room again. Crane had written OLLIE STRINGER on the chart and ADRIAN with a question mark, while telling them what Ollie had told him. Anderson listened with the crooked grin Crane was getting to know only too well. He'd studied a lot of body language in his time and he could tell that the reporter's was beginning to tense.

'I could have gone along too, Frank. I could have made time last night.'

'I had to work on him to get him to speak to *me*. If I'd gone round there with a crime reporter he'd have been a write-off.' Crane spoke more tersely than he'd intended. He was beginning to hate it, having to explain the way he worked, to write it all down, to know that Anderson was intent on controlling everything.

But Anderson began slowly nodding. 'It's a valid point.' Then he put on one of his practised smiles in the old engaging way. 'Well done, pal. I can see I've got a lot to learn from an expert like you.'

'Just experience, that's all. In this game you often find

yourself going over well-trodden ground and so you have to learn to look closer.'

There was a great deal more to it than that, but Crane knew they were exerting themselves to meet each other halfway, as they each had so much the other needed: Anderson's knowledge of the case and Crane's ability in the field. Even so, Crane was anxious to reach an answer to Donna's killing before the reporter, if it were possible for anyone to. His pride was now very much involved in what Anderson clearly regarded as a competition.

Anderson said, 'This Adrian guy makes my nose twitch.'

'And mine.'

'But would Donna have gone out with an AC/DC?' he said, pulling a face. 'What do you think, Patsy? HIV-wise, it might have been dodgy.'

'There wasn't much she didn't know about safe sex,' she said. 'And anyway she might not have twigged what he was.'

Crane felt it could quite easily become near impossible for Anderson to attempt to profile Donna as the sweet innocent she'd looked if he ever did get to write that final story. He said, 'Why might a bisexual have reason to kill her?'

'Blackmail again?' Anderson scribbled on the sheet now devoted to Adrian. 'Maybe he's married and his wife doesn't know he's AC/DC, and might have given him the welly if she'd found out.'

'Bias at work if it came to light? It still happens.'

'Perhaps another gay,' Patsy said. 'Jealous of Adrian going out with a woman.'

'Nice one, Patsy,' Crane said. Pleased, she began to redden.

'But gays tend not to do violence,' Anderson said.

'Joe Orton wouldn't have thought so.'

'When do you aim to see Ollie again?' The reporter spoke tentatively.

Crane also forced tact. 'Tomorrow evening. We could both go, now he trusts me. You can be a colleague. He'll take to a bloke with your looks.'

'Bugger! I'm tied up. Can't get out of it either. It's an Asian girl being forced into a marriage against her will. She's on the run and she's made very complex arrangements to see me and talk about it. You couldn't make it the evening after?'

'Sorry. I've promised Ollie and it's too hot a lead. I'll make sure it all goes on your flip chart.'

That wasn't the point, but Anderson smiled in cheerful resignation. 'I've got to go now, but keep up the good work, Frank, and *do* keep me in touch, said he with a mirthless grin.'

'That Geoff,' Patsy said, shaking her head as the door closed on him. She gave Crane a conspiratorial smile. 'Do you want *my* news now?'

He watched in silence as she opened a handbag and took out a small black diary. It was stamped in gold with the initials DJ.

'No!'

'I made another search of her room. I felt all round the edge of the carpet, but there were no loose bits anywhere. So I looked at the drawers in the base of her bed again. I knew the police had had everything out, but something made me feel underneath. The diary was in an envelope and she'd fastened that to the underside of one of the drawers, right at the back, with Scotch tape. She'd have been worried any of us might lay hands on it.'

'Well *done*, Patsy! I don't think even the police would think she was going to keep a diary so well hidden. Bloody well done!'

'You'll soon see why she kept it so well hidden,' she sad sadly. 'And it might not help much.'

Crane quickly saw why. His elation ebbed. It wasn't a record of where she'd been and who with. She'd written down initials and figures only, the figures entered neatly beside the initials, in brackets. £75 seemed to be the going rate. It could be less and it could be a lot more, especially on Saturdays. Sometimes the letter B would show up with the letter F at the side, also in brackets. A figure would be entered each Sunday that checked out as the week's takings, which was rarely fewer than three amounts. He turned to the little accounting section at the back. He found that this had been kept just as meticulously, weekly totals brought forward and added into monthlies. There was a regular figure included in the weekly amounts of £170, which he took to be Donna's net pay from Leaf and Petal. Detailed expenses were also accounted for: motor, HP, clothes, hair, make-up, house and so on. There was always a healthy bottom line.

They looked at each other. 'Couldn't do sums to save her life when she was at school,' she said flatly. 'Seemed to have learnt fast.'

'Money's a fast teacher. There seems to be a lot of money left over, according to this. Six grand at least. Know if she had a cheque account?'

'She always swore she didn't have enough to make it worthwhile. Told Mam and Dad she found it impossible to save. She only gave them a tiny bit towards her board.'

'So what happened to the money, Patsy?'

'Could have had it with her. Could have been killed for it.'

'It's a good idea, but can you see anyone as careful as she was carrying thousands of pounds around in a handbag?'

'You're right. She was so careful with everything.'

'But if all this money's gone it gives the case an extra angle.'

'I could have another scout round in her bedroom.'

'Might be worth it. The police weren't looking for money, they'd assume she had none, like most teenagers.'

She nodded ruefully at the little book. 'It can only mean one thing, can't it?'

'It's got to be sex for cash. Apart from B. I'd guess B stood for Bobby and he seemed to qualify for a freebie. It looked as if she made Bobby pay by winding him up rotten.'

She gazed despondently out over the unkempt strip of lawn and the peeling garages. He guessed she found it very hard to equate the near call girl Donna looked to have become with the little sister she'd helped to bathe and dress, and played with in the wendy house.

Crane looked back at the diary. The letter C appeared regularly. 'Could C stand for Clive Fletcher, do you think?'

'He was trying to get her into modelling,' she said doubtfully. 'They say he always expects it to come free from the girls he's looking after.'

'Well, he's paid here and that could have been something that bugged him. And A crops up in the months before she died. Could that be Adrian? There's also a J that figures a lot. Often at the weekend, with amounts of a hundred or more, but other times showing no figure at all.

Interesting. Could mean she stayed the night somewhere. Was she away much at weekends?'

'When wasn't she? She'd go to the garden centre on Saturdays and take her going out clothes with her. She was always with her friend Pam if anyone wanted to know.'

'Pam covered for her?'

'The police talked to her, but she had no more idea where Donna got to than I did.'

'Surely she'd not be as secretive as that with her best mate.'

'Pam kept her neb out, just thought herself lucky Donna *was* her best mate. She was nothing like as pretty as Donna, no one was, but being around her meant she got to get Donna's leavings.' It was a symbiosis as old as time, the plain one and the pretty one, and she spoke with a resigned bitterness.

Crane gave the diary a final glance. There were other initials scattered through the pages, but the ones that appeared regularly were B, C, A and J. 'I'll tell Ted Benson you've found this, they'll need it when they make a fresh start.' But he knew the police would be as disappointed as he was that it hadn't been a regular diary, with full names and an account of her movements.

'I'll get you a drink,' she said. 'You shouldn't have brought that bag of booze.' She looked at him gratefully. It was clear no one else had ever brought her a bag of booze, let alone flowers or scent.

He shrugged. 'You can't afford to keep giving out free drinks. Why didn't you dig out the diary when Geoff was here?'

'I ... wanted you to see it first,' she said, reddening again. 'So you could decide what to do before he starts trying to take over, like he always does.'

She was a bright kid. She'd picked up on the tension both men tried to conceal behind a jokey manner. 'It doesn't seem fair,' she said, 'you're finding out these new things and I have a feeling he wants to take the credit for them if you get anywhere. He's a good looking bloke and you can't help liking him, but good lookers can be very self-centred.'

Crane thought that she'd know if anyone did, having had a sister like Donna. He took her lightly by the shoulders. 'He's pushy and he's driven, Patsy, but all that really matters is finding your sister's killer.' He could have added that the worst vibes he got from Anderson were that he'd damage the case by his impetuosity, his lack of tact, and his gnawing ambition to get down to Fleet Street, or Wapping, or wherever the big papers hung out these days.

'You keep an eye on him, Frank.'

He took his hands away, sensing that she'd have liked him to keep them there. She smiled uncertainly and went off for the drinks. Crane was pushed for time but felt he had to spend another ten or fifteen minutes with her. It gave her such a boost to have them there, him and Anderson, that was obvious. They made her feel useful and needed in those flip chart sessions and it had been like transferring a wilting plant into the right kind of soil. Poor kid, plain maybe yet comely and intelligent. But simply neglected in a house where her glamorous little sister had hoovered up all the attention.

When she came back with the drinks, they sat on the sofa. She was still in a state of animation and it was beginning to be hard to remember her as the drab and apathetic woman he'd first seen.

'I … saw the personnel lady today,' she said. 'Asked her if they'd bear me in mind for supervising work. She seemed really pleased. She said they'd already considered me because I was a good worker, but they'd thought I didn't want the responsibility.'

'What did I tell you? You've got to push yourself, you see. No one else will.' But he knew the altered hairstyle had swung it and the modest make-up and the growing confidence. 'Good work, Patsy!'

'She said as soon as there's a vacancy they'll talk to me about it.'

'There you are then. And once you've got on the next rung keep going. You've got the intelligence and the ability, you've already shown that in the help you've given me.'

When he'd gone she sat over her drink, thinking how much she was beginning to enjoy life. She couldn't believe how dreary everything had seemed before Frank Crane had come into it. He was so encouraging, so keen to see her make a new start. And he knew she was trying hard with her hair and her clothes, it was the sort of thing you could tell by the way he looked you over. She wanted to go on wondering about Frank but hardly dared. She was sure he lived alone as he seemed to work all the time. That smile of his, that he was so mean with. When he gave her that smile it made her insides flutter. And when he'd put his hands on her shoulders …!

As Crane drove away he felt his sense of guilt beginning to lift. Poor kid, he'd only taken a drink with her that first time because he'd realized how useful she could be to him. But there'd been a plus side for her too that made him feel better about using her. He knew she fancied him, but there was nothing he could do about that. It would have to be sorted out at the right time.

It had been an overcast day of intense humidity. Crane, forehead beaded in sweat, climbed the steps again to the upper reservoir. He seemed to be breathing air as dense as liquid. He expected to see Ollie's straw hat the moment he reached the top, but he wasn't at his bench yet. He sat down and waited. There seemed to be no one else about just now and the only sound was echoing birdsong.

Five minutes slowly passed. It seemed odd when he was said to be 'always around'. Maybe the heat was getting to him. He wondered if he'd have anything to pass on. It could be the breakthrough: a bisexual who knew the area backwards, whose name hadn't been picked up by the police because the gays didn't talk to police, combined with Donna's own obsessive secrecy.

He then heard a sound that was different from the rest. It was a noise like a thin cry of pain, as if one animal was attacking another. He heard the cry again. It could have been anything. He had no feel for woodland life. It could almost have been human. He stood up uneasily, the fine hairs stiffening along his bare arms. The sound had come from directly behind him. He began to move warily over dry ground, through patches of dense fern and the leaf mould of decades, into a deeply shaded hollow.

Ollie lay in the middle of the hollow. His head oozed blood and his bloodstained Panama hat lay a yard away. There was so much blood it was difficult to see the actual wounds. A red bubble formed on his open mouth. A shattered arm lay motionless at one side of his plump body, his other arm twitched sluggishly. He gave another of the tiny moaning cries Crane had heard from the bench.

He shook his head, his emotions torn between pity and guilt. Pity for a harmless gay who'd suddenly wanted to know too much, and guilt because had it not been for him he'd still be on his bench, looking forward to a nice gossip and the chance to get laid.

He took out his mobile.

'How's he doing?'

Benson pursed his lips. 'Damn near a flatline, but the poor sod's still alive, just. Want my opinion, he was left for dead.'

'When do you think he'll be able to speak?'

'Couple of weeks if he's lucky. His jaw's so badly broken it'll have to be wired. And even when he can talk he's not going to. Not to us. You know what they're like. What's the story?'

'There's a bisexual lurking about somewhere called Adrian. Could be connected to the Donna killing. I gave Ollie a twenty to see if he could come up with anything.' He gave him the rest of the details.

Benson watched him. Crane could sense his resentment that he'd contrived to get a contact in the gay reservoir community, not that it had done any good yet. Cruisers didn't speak to the police was the accepted wisdom, but Crane knew that Benson knew that even if he had not lost his job in the force he'd still have found a way.

'Think someone warned this Adrian?'

'It could be looking that way.'

'Well, the gays are going to *have* to do some talking

now,' Benson said grimly. 'They either talk or we apply to close the place down after six. That should give them the message.' He finished his half of bitter. 'Well, I'll be off. Christ, I'm not scratching around for something to do just now, what with Mr Blobby getting done over and Terry gearing up to make a fresh start on the Donna carry-on.' He hesitated, then said with reluctance, 'Thanks for the tip-off about Marvin Jackson, by the way. We had him in, told him he either coughed about the guns or we treated him as a leading suspect in Donna's case. He coughed.'

Crane watched him go. Shrugged. He knew Terry Jones would have leant on Benson to make sure he showed Crane due gratitude. They'd been in it together, he and Benson, the evidence-planting against a villain who took up more police time than a quarter of the other rubbish, and was simply the most evil, loathsome human being Crane had ever known. And Crane had taken the fall because of Benson's kids and sick wife. And that wouldn't have been so bad if Benson could have accepted the favour, if he'd not somehow, in his mind, begun to think he'd come out of it with clean hands and that Crane had been responsible for the lot. The mind was a funny thing. Crane also knew that if he'd acted alone in the evidence-planting, seen to every detail himself, it wouldn't have come to light. But Benson had been his best friend and had wanted to help.

It was flip chart time again. Ollie's battering was already front page news in the *Standard*, but Crane gave them his horse's mouth version, scribbling the details of Ollie's sad fate on his own sheet. 'It could have been you as well, Frank!' Patsy said in shocked tones, grasping his arm. 'He could still have been around, whoever it was.'

'No way, Patsy,' Anderson said sombrely. 'They don't hang about when they've given someone that kind of belting. They leg it fast.'

It was only the second time Crane had seen the reporter's mobile face so still. He was bitterly disappointed. 'The poor sod must have been asking too many questions, too suddenly and in too many faces.'

'And it got around fast. Well, he's still breathing, just, but he's never going to talk to anyone again. About anything.'

'And the police'll get nothing out of the others, whatever they do. Not now.' Anderson sipped his drink despondently. 'Christ, I never even made it to the SOC. My sidekick covered it. I was with the Asian girl at a safe house in Doncaster.'

Crane sensed that what really bugged him was being caught between two good stories, rather than poor Ollie's sickening injuries, while Crane struggled with the guilt of involving the poor guy. 'Well,' he said, sighing, 'that about brings us up to speed, apart from one final matter. Patsy made another toothcomb search of Donna's room at home and found something the police missed. A diary.'

'A diary?' he cried. 'A *diary*! One that ...' He let the sentence dangle in his excitement, suddenly so keyed up that his hand shook.

'Chill out,' Crane told him, with a wry smile. 'It tells us just one thing, that she was on the game big time. Nothing else.'

'Can I see it? You've not handed it over to Benson and Co?'

'Not yet. We'll have to, soon. Patsy's still got it here.'

She handed it to him and the reporter, hands still trembling, flicked rapidly through the weeks leading up to her death, studying the items intently, just as Crane had done. It soon became clear he'd reached the same conclusion.

'What became of the loot?'

'You tell us.'

'She really was putting it about, wasn't she?'

'I've been thinking about it. I'd say she was pacing herself. She was charging top dollar too, top dollar in Bradford terms anyway, and she was accounting for the money very carefully. It was as if she had a long-term plan.'

Anderson flicked ruefully through the pages one last time. Donna's background and way of life had been his obsession. He'd known she mixed with unsavoury types. But Donna's obsession had been secrecy and Crane didn't think the reporter had even begun to guess at the highly organized call girl she'd made of herself. Crane guessed that he now saw that big concluding feature shredding before his eyes, of a Donna he'd just about been able to pass off as an ingenuous teenager corrupted by the men she'd come up against, her fate sealed by the accident of being born on the Willows. If anyone ever *was* brought to trial for her murder, the defence wouldn't hesitate to imply that she'd been partly to blame for her own death by the company she'd chosen to keep. Crane couldn't forget Patsy's words as she'd sat in his car the first night they'd met. 'She asked for it, Frank.'

'Well, where do we go from here?' Anderson said heavily.

'My feeling is we talk to Fletcher and Hellewell. She spent a lot of time with both of them. We could ask if she mentioned an Adrian. We could also test out their own alibis. Let's start with Fletcher. You know him, you've talked to him. When would be a good time to catch him?'

'Early evening, at home. Definitely at home.' He began to find his old cocky grin. 'That bugs him. He's frightened about his wife finding out about the porno stuff. I reckon she's an important part of his back-up: humping gear for the weddings, chatting people up and selling the service, all that. Comes from a respectable county family. Fletcher answers the door himself and rushes you upstairs. He has an office up there, plus a studio and darkroom. She'll know about the routine modelling for the catalogues but I'm certain she's in the dark about the basement he rents and what goes on down there.'

'This basement—'

'Spent hours checking it out. Warehouse building in the Old Quarter. I've seen young girls and blokes go down there. I've shadowed one or two of the kids, tried chatting them up in the Glass-house, no chance. The money's good and he backs it up with threats, and they know he means what he says. The police know what he's up to but they have no proof, and anyway it comes so far behind the city's drugs problem as to be out of sight.'

Crane gave a respectful nod. He'd certainly done his leg work. 'Do you think he could have used Donna in a porn video?'

'No. He's nobody's fool. He was certain he could agent her to the fashion industry. If she didn't make it legit the blue movies would have been a fall-back.'

Crane glanced at Patsy, who gave a resigned shrug. Again, it was more or less what she too had said on the first night. 'What say we drop in on him tomorrow evening, around seven, if you're free?'

'I'll be in the Glass-house after six. I'll ring you if I can't make it.'

When he'd gone Patsy made Crane another drink and they sat on the sofa. 'I do hope you find someone, Frank.'

'Me too. And Mr Pushy deserves a break, he's never stopped working on it. I know he's only thinking in terms of his career, but I suppose that's what ambitious journalists are like. And it's Geoff's ambition that might very well get us there in the end.'

Though Crane was determined that he was going to get there first, he was aware that he was up against someone with investigative skills almost as sharp as his own, and who took any mistakes as badly as he did. But then he had to remind himself that he and Anderson weren't opponents, they were supposed to be on the same side.

'How are things going at work, Patsy?'

She coloured slightly, in the familiar way. 'Nancy, one of the supervisors, asked me to sit with her during my lunch break. She began telling me what my duties would be if I got promoted.'

'That means you will be.'

'She said she was sure I'd do well, because I know all the girls and get on with them.'

'She'll know.'

'Trouble is, the girls have sussed what's going on. They're not the same. I mean they're still friendly, but they seem to be watching what they're saying, know what I mean?'

'You'll never really be one of them again, not if you're going to be over them. But you'll make new friends, on the next rung.'

She nodded dejectedly. It was the first time her new-found enthusiasm for getting on seemed to have deserted her. Crane was glad to turn away for a time from the mind-numbing problems surrounding her sister's death, to help someone with problems of her own.

Carol was sitting in the Glass-house with several of her colleagues. 'Hi,' she said. 'Touching base with the cave man?'

Crane sat next to her. 'You know that cliché "the usual suspects"? Well, we're aiming to talk to them all over again.'

'That's more like it,' she said, grinning, 'we get *such* a petted lip when you will keep doing things without him.'

'So I'm finding out.'

'Trouble is, he's always seen it as *his* story and he gets very agitated about anyone trying to share it. We all tend to get a bit proprietorial in this business. He probably thinks you might want to write a book about it.'

'He's the writer, not me. And anyway, he deserves whatever he can make out of the Donna Jackson story. No one could have worked harder on it than him.'

'Don't I know it. He's spent so much time on it I was beginning to wonder if there was a bit on the side involved. These people you keep talking to, I don't suppose one of them's female, gorgeous-looking and giving him googoo eyes?' She giggled to imply she was only joking, but he could tell she was speaking in code and making a serious request. He shook his head.

'Women didn't seem to figure much in Donna's life. So far, it's been blokes all the way.'

She looked relieved, but Crane knew she was always going to have worries about Anderson and other women, because wherever he was the eyes of other women followed him.

'What I'll do when he runs off to London I can't imagine,' she said. 'I'll be up against girls who have double firsts and work in television and earn a million a year. But will they be able to cook, I ask myself, or change a duvet cover, or programme a DVD-recorder?' She was giggling again, and Crane felt that what she was saying now was that she could turn a blind eye to Anderson having the occasional affair as long as he always came back to her. He knew from experience that some women could live with this state of affairs around men of looks and charm who showed every sign of having a glowing future.

Then her green eyes softened and he knew Anderson stood behind him before he felt his hand on his shoulder. 'You need to watch this one, Carol,' Anderson said breezily. 'These quiet types with their sympathetic smiles can be inside your knickers while you're still telling them how you felt when the dog died.'

'I did try to warn him how insanely jealous you get. Anyway, who said I had any knickers on?'

He squeezed in at the table, giving her the sort of smile that went with a private joke. 'One drink and then off, Frank?'

'I'll get them. Carol?'

'Can we go in your car? It's best if we don't seem to roll up mob-handed. Not with Fletcher.'

'I'll drive yours to the flat, Geoff, if you like,' Carol said. 'It'll save Frank having to come back into town. I can leave mine at the office.'

The hesitation was almost imperceptible but it was

there. 'Oh … good idea, Carol. We'll have a bite to eat when I get back.'

It confirmed what Crane had suspected. Anderson was getting bored with her. Maybe her instincts were sound and there *was* another woman on the go.

He lived on the old Keighley-Skipton road. The house was large, elegant and Edwardian and at the rear overlooked open country. Ornamental trees dotted a garden that was mainly lawn with well-kept borders. Fletcher was clearly doing well.

Shadows were lengthening in the evening sun as they walked up the drive. Anderson drew the handle of an old-fashioned bell pull. The door was opened very quickly. He gave Crane's unknown face a wary glance before looking at Anderson. 'Oh, you again,' he said, in a low hard tone. 'Well you can forget it. I've already told you everything I knew about her.'

'There's been a development, Mr Fletcher,' Anderson said courteously, with his warm smile. 'Could you possibly spare us a few minutes?'

'No.'

'I'm a private investigator, Mr Fletcher,' Crane said. 'Frank Crane, working for Donna's parents. It would be a great help to me, and them, if we could spend a little time with you.'

'Who is it, Clive?' a woman's voice called.

'Oh, shit,' he muttered. 'You'd better come in.'

They moved into a large square hall. The woman looked from a half-open door and the hall smelt faintly of good cooking. 'Two gentlemen wanting to arrange a portrait of their board of directors,' he told her, with well-honed presence of mind. 'I'll take them up to the office.'

'Right you are.' She gave them a friendly smile. 'I can hold dinner.' She was fortyish, plumpish, and had rather coarse, tinted-blonde hair. A slight vagueness seemed to go with the pleasant manner. Crane felt it was a vagueness that would be of great help to Fletcher in living his double life under her nose.

They followed him up a wide staircase. It had dark oak balustrades that also ran along a lengthy landing. Two teenage girls hung over the landing rail and gazed lingeringly at Anderson before going back to their rooms. Anderson glanced at Crane with a small upward jerk of his head. It translated as two pretty young kids whose father made obscene movies of pretty young kids.

Fletcher led them over creaking floorboards and through a door at the end of the landing. This was his office. It had doors to left and right, which Crane guessed were studio and darkroom. It was comfortably furnished and had a large antique pedestal desk and a bow-back Windsor chair. Lavish examples of his highly-skilled work were displayed on the walls: wedding groups in dappled sunlight, winsome babies, family portraits, businessmen looking decisive.

'Well, get on with it,' he said tersely.

'Things have changed, Mr Fletcher,' Crane told him. 'It was common knowledge that Bobby Mahon was the leading suspect in Donna's murder. He's now been cleared.'

Crane saw a flicker of unease in his eyes, but otherwise he gave little away. He was about five-ten and well-built, with strong features and a head of thick auburn hair. His eyes were dark blue and glinted when they caught the light, and seemed to hint at the faint, louche lassitude of a man overdrawing on sizeable energy levels. Crane guessed he overdid everything: work, play, drink, sex. He'd certainly have access to plenty of sex.

'You'd better sit,' he said, with an edginess he could only just control. 'Christ, I never thought it could be anyone else but that shithead.'

'These things happen, sir,' Anderson said comfortingly.

'It means the police have to make a fresh start,' Crane told him.

'Does that mean I'll have to waste time with them too?'

'If we can get a firm lead on Donna's killer we should be able to spare you any further dealings with DS Benson.'

'I spent a lot of time with that kid,' he said harshly. 'She had the most photogenic face I've ever pointed a lens at. I could have made her a big name. Apart from that I liked her, liked her a lot.'

Enough to shell out seventy-odd pounds a throw to sleep with her? Crane wondered if he really was the C in her diary. But then Fletcher suddenly had a haunted look about him, as if his unfocused eyes saw again the woman he'd photographed so often. He looked forlorn, as if he genuinely grieved.

'Oh, well,' Anderson said gently, 'at least you've got plenty of other attractive young women to console yourself with.'

'What's that supposed to mean?' he snapped, back in the present, eyes glinting, face hard.

'Your glamour photography. Your remarkable ability to make young women look their sexy best. You very kindly lent us a picture of Donna to put in the paper when the poor kid's body was found, remember?'

The other watched him. He couldn't quite decide if he

was being needled by this amiable young man, but Crane was quite certain he was. It was Mahon and pointing the bone all over again.

'Just to get things straight in my own mind, sir,' Crane said. 'Would you mind telling me when you last saw Donna?'

'Two days before she went missing,' he said mechanically. 'We'd had another long photo shoot. Pros, we need dozens of shots to get the right one.'

'And they were all … routine modelling shots?' Anderson asked, with subtly pointed emphasis.

'Of course they bloody were!' he said, stung. 'That's the only kind of glamour work I *do*.'

Crane and Anderson both knew the value of a dubious silence and they let it roll for a few seconds. Crane said, 'Did Donna ever mention an Adrian, sir? It's very important. No surname, I'm afraid.'

He seemed genuinely to be searching his memory. He finally shook his head. 'Means nothing. She talked about Mahon now and then, and the guy who owns Leaf and Petal – Joe Hellewell – but that's about it.'

Crane nodded. 'I know the police have gone into all this, but would you mind telling me where you were the night Donna went missing?'

'The Photographic Society dinner at the Norfolk Gardens.'

'About what time did it end?'

'Elevenish.'

'And you came directly home?'

'Yes. My wife can vouch …' He'd said it all before.

'In your own motor?'

He gave the slightest pause. '… Yes.'

'Wasn't that rather unusual?'

'Why should it be? I'd only had a couple.'

'Oh ...' Crane shrugged. 'I suppose if I'd gone to a boozy do I'd have wanted to get a few down and join in the fun. I'd have taken a taxi.'

Crane heard Anderson's soft intake of breath as a second flicker of anxiety showed in Fletcher's glinting eyes. He wasn't ready for this, it had caught him off his guard. It had to have been a question neither the police nor Anderson had thought to put.

'Taxis, they're ... expensive from this distance,' he said uneasily.

Crane glanced pointedly at his Rolex, his handmade cotton shirt and silk tie. Fletcher didn't like it, that he'd looked to need to raid the petty cash tin.

'Ten miles,' Crane said musingly. '£25 return?'

'I went in my own *car*, what's the big deal?'

He was flushing with irritation, because though sharp he'd not seen this coming. Anderson had though. The big deal was that Crane couldn't believe a wealthy man who liked a drink would spend four hours nursing two. Unless he needed to stay sober to drive on from the dinner to see a girlfriend. A girlfriend who'd possibly been eased into a reservoir.

'Were your daughters at home that night, sir?'

His colour deepened slightly. 'I ... can't remember. What's that got to do with anything? Christ, it's twelve months ago.'

In other words they'd been away. Crane wondered if he might be on to something, felt a familiar frisson. It meant his wife would be home alone. What if Fletcher had given her a doctored drink before he'd set off to his dinner, which had meant she'd slept so soundly she'd had no real idea when he'd crept under the duvet?

The phone rang. Fletcher snatched it up, listened. 'Oh, all right,' he said slowly, glancing at the two men. 'Look, I'll take it in the drawing room, Steph.' He put down the phone, said to Crane, 'Give me five, but when I get back we'll need to wrap this up PDQ. My family want their dinner.' He went off.

'What can it be he wants neither us or his missus to hear?' Anderson said, chuckling. 'Had the arsehole on the run there, didn't you, Crane? Bugger, why didn't *I* think to ask him how he'd got to the Norfolk?'

He wore his usual wry smile, but Crane now knew the intense irritation it was concealing in a man as aggressively competitive as Anderson. Crane couldn't help feeling amused to have got ahead of him once again, but simply said, 'If you were a PI and not a newspaperman you'd have picked up on it.' It was true. He missed out on very little as it was.

The reporter winked, stood up. 'Well, the cat's away. He might not have locked *everything* up.' He began to try drawers, without success, then turned to an outsize filing cabinet. 'Ha ha, he's overlooked this, but it just seems to be file copies of his prints. Let's try J for Jackson, shall we?'

'This might not be a good idea. If he catches you he'll have us straight through the door.'

'Oh, come on, Frank. We cut corners, blokes like us. Let's see what kinds of shots he was really taking of her. Those creaking floorboards on the landing should warn us when he's on his way back.'

It was this kind of impulsiveness in Anderson that Crane had always been so uneasy about, but he had to admit to being curious. Anyway, he was already leafing through a wad of glossy prints. They all seemed to be totally respectable modelling shots. They showed Donna right profile, left profile, full face. Donna in even light, in shadow, in a key light that gave emphasis to those luminous round eyes with their riveting impression of an innocence that blended with depth, emotion with spirituality. Donna in black and white, in colour, in a sepia tint. Donna standing, sitting, lying down, even twirling, arms extended as gracefully as the wings of a planing bird, gleaming hair flying about her like a fully opened fan.

'God, what a cracker she was,' Anderson muttered.

It said it all, that such a pretty and vibrant woman should have had such an appalling fate. Crane felt he could sympathize then with the journalist's urge to profile her as the guileless creature she'd certainly looked. The sad symbolic victim of an upbringing in a sink estate. Even though he'd always known the description wasn't going to fit.

And then Anderson turned up a print showing Donna naked.

She stood framed by a half-open door, and looking away from the lens, as if unaware of it, her impossibly perfect rounded breasts slightly suspended as she leant forward, apparently to pick up pants and bra, hair now cascading down the sides of her flawless features, her belly flat, her legs smooth and slender, her waist so narrow it looked as if it could easily be encircled by a pair of male hands.

The floorboards didn't creak. Fletcher, paranoid, must have tiptoed. He was in the room before the folder could even be closed. He took it all in in a nano-second. 'I'll speak to your editor in the morning, Anderson,' he rasped. 'You'll be wise to start clearing your desk. And you, Crane, you should know better. Don't think you'll get away with it either.'

But Anderson gave him a relaxed smile. 'You'll not be doing any of that, Mr Fletcher. You'll be too worried. You see, this is a print of a naked young woman you were supposed to be grooming for a modelling career. She subsequently ended up in a reservoir. Was that because she'd not agree to go in that cellar of yours with the soft lights on and her fanny in the air? Or maybe she'd got to know too much?'

Fletcher was flushed brick red. 'Any more on those lines, mister, and you'll be in a court room before you can spit.'

'Mr Fletcher,' Crane said quietly, 'if the police could find the time and the evidence you'd be in a court room yourself. They certainly know about your cellar and your obscene videos and your use of underage people.'

'She didn't know I'd taken it, you dozy sods!' he suddenly cried. 'Well, look at them, they're all standard poses except one. *That* one. She didn't know I'd taken it. She was changing into normal gear. She'd left the door open. I couldn't resist it. She didn't even *know*, for Christ's sake. She didn't …' He broke off in a voice that seemed almost choked by a sob.

Crane believed him. It was obvious he was speaking off the cuff. He'd taken a single shot, charming in its artfulness, of a naked beauty dressing herself. Shades of Renoir.

'But we can't be sure where it led to, Mr Fletcher, can we?' Anderson said softly, smile still intact.

'I'll have to pass on what we've learnt here to the police,

sir,' Crane told him, 'because I think you went on some-where after the Norfolk dinner, and I think they'll want to go into that with you again. I'd try to be very, very coop-erative, if I were you.'

'And we'll need to keep this print,' Anderson said calmly, storing it in what seemed to be a specially enlarged inside pocket of his lightweight jacket.

'Don't you dare!' Fletcher screamed, rushing at him. 'Don't you bloody dare! It's my property and it only leaves here under warrant.'

'And give you the chance to destroy it and the negative? Dear me, you must think I was brought up in Barnsley, Mr Fletcher ... sir.'

Fletcher seized him by his jacket lapels. It wasn't a wise move. Without a word, Anderson pushed him off and gave him a single blow to the chest. It was all it needed. Hunched over, gasping for breath, Fletcher almost crawled to his Windsor chair and flopped into it. He looked tough, and almost certainly was, he'd been simply outclassed. Crane guessed that most people would be around Anderson.

'So sorry, Mr Fletcher,' he said, affable as ever. 'I always try my best to keep things civil. You really mustn't trouble to show us out.'

Crane drove back to Bradford along the bypass, through peaceful meadowland, with views of a range of hills purpling in setting sunlight.

Anderson said, 'What do you think?'

'I'm positive he went on somewhere from the Norfolk.'

'All right, brains, don't rub it in.'

The wry smile was there, but he was still brooding and tense about Crane picking up on the oddness of Fletcher driving himself to a booze up. The reporter had to be just about the most competitive man he'd ever known.

'But I can't see it being him,' Crane went on. 'He's a shrewd businessman, he'd spent hours on her as an investment. If she took off in the glossies she could be worth a million a year, fifteen, twenty per cent to him, yes? I also think he was levelling about the nude print.'

Crane swung his Megane off the bypass and on to a roundabout that would put them on the Bradford Road. Out of the corner of his eye he saw the reporter nod.

'I guess you're right,' Anderson said, with a sigh. 'Still, we gave the slimy sod's feathers a good ruffling, didn't we?'

'And if he's right in the head he'll close the cellar overnight, so that's a plus.'

Crane dropped him off at his flat in Frizinghall. It was a good one in one of the many converted wool-baron mansions. He glimpsed curly black hair and an eager smile at a window, but Anderson reacted with an indifference you could only just detect. Crane had to concede that you had special problems if you looked like Anderson, with every woman in sight fluttering her eyes at you. He drove on to Conway House, where he was to pick up Patsy and to drive on to Connie and Malc's semi.

'I think we can probably rule out Fletcher,' he told Patsy, when she was sitting in the car. 'And he doesn't know of an Adrian. We're aiming to see Hellewell tomorrow.'

'If only it wasn't so long ago. Whoever did it could be hundreds of miles away by now.'

'Killers often stick around, Patsy, for one reason or another. Their jobs or their families. Take your friendly, neighbourhood Yorkshire Ripper …'

It was dark now and the Willows looked slightly more attractive in the glow of lighted windows. The closely parked cars didn't look quite as decrepit when you couldn't see the scuffs and dints and balding tyres. But bands of cat-calling youths roamed the narrow roads or hung about on corners.

'God,' Patsy said, 'I wish we could have been brought up in a nice house on a private estate. Maybe Donna wouldn't …'

Crane put a hand briefly over hers. He didn't believe it would have made a scrap of difference where Donna had been brought up. She was a one-off.

'Only me, Mam,' Patsy said, as she and Crane stood at the door of the tiny living room of number 27. 'Frank's with me.'

They both looked up in anxious expectancy. Crane's presence usually involved some kind of drama. 'Frank just wants to have a shufti at Donna's room,' Patsy told them. 'Thinks there just might be something the police missed.'

'There's … no news then?' Malc asked nervously.

'Not so far, Malc. But we're talking again to the people who spent time with Donna. Me and Geoff Anderson, that is. He's being a great help, he knows so much of the background. And he's very dedicated.' Because of the story, he thought grimly, that rather cosy word the press employed even for the starkest of human tragedies.

'He's a good lad,' Connie said, lamplight etching the hollows in her gaunt face. 'He was very kind to us.'

'We'll just pop upstairs, then,' Patsy said. 'Shan't be long.'

'You're looking very posh again, love,' Malc said. 'Going out later?'

She reddened, shook her head. They both looked puzzled. It seemed to be a Patsy they couldn't fully adjust to, having been used to one who'd slopped around in old clothes, hair everywhere, looking depressed. She wore a crisply ironed, embroidered shell top and pale blue trousers, and the soft fall of her hair shone from the care she was taking of it. Crane's guilt about using her had finally lifted, as it hadn't been a one-way street. The problem now was that though he'd got to like her a lot as a friend, she was showing the unmistakeable signs of a woman who was clearly hoping it was going to be a lot more than that.

'Well, you look very nice, love,' Connie said. Crane wished they could have paid her more compliments in the days when any colour she might have had was constantly bleached out by Donna's incredible radiance.

Donna's bedroom was papered in lemon, with floral tie-back curtains. The overhead globe had a pleated uplighter and there was a silk-shaded lamp on the bedside cupboard, a radio and a slender vase that held a single artificial amaryllis. The carpet was gold coloured with a white fleecy rug at the bedside. The built-in wardrobe combined a tiny dressing table and there was a small armchair in a corner. The room was spotlessly clean and gave off a delicate apple scent.

Patsy gave a crooked grin. 'Her room got most of the attention.' She ran a hand over a crisp duvet cover. 'She nattered for things, wheedled with those big eyes. They always gave in, gave her whatever she wanted. Mam was never done paying off the catalogue.'

'When it looks as if she could have bought herself anything she wanted. She's got to have done *something* with the money.'

'I've searched and better searched.'

Crane looked in the wardrobe. It was crammed: tops, skirts, trousers, jackets, dresses, a raincoat, a winter coat, a parka. The police, and Patsy, would have checked all the pockets. 'This parka looks almost new,' he said in a musing tone.

'She hated coats. Even in winter she'd rush out in a thin jacket. Mam bought the coats, she was so worried she'd catch her death, but would madam wear them? Never saw her in the parka once, even when it was sub-zero.'

He drew out the parka. It seemed slightly heavier than he might have expected. He felt the hem. It seemed thicker than normal but could have been the way the padding was arranged. He pulled out the material of the inside pocket. The stitching was intact and seemed tamper free. 'Was Donna good with a needle and thread?'

'Very. Blouses, dresses, T-shirts, nothing was ever quite right for her. She'd spend hours unpicking and resewing. I think it was her only real hobby. Well,' she said wryly, 'that and screwing.'

'Mind if I cut open the inside pocket?'

'Mam'll never know.'

He snipped it carefully open with his folding scissors, then slipped a hand down between coat and lining to touch thin, compact bundles of what felt like banknotes, resting along the hem. Patsy gasped as he eased one out. New fifties, secured with elastic bands. He counted the first bundle gingerly, trying to touch the surfaces as little as possible. There were twenty. The other bundles looked to be the same. 'A bit up on the diary total,' he told her. 'Seven grand.'

'*Seven grand*! And giving Mam a tenner a week for her keep!'

Crane took out a large plastic bag, put in the notes, sealed it. 'The police will need to run them past their forensic people, there could be something that might help. Your folks should be told. The money will be theirs, and yours, when it's returned.'

'They'd not be able to handle it, Frank, not if it came from screwing. They'd never use it. I'd not be surprised if Dad didn't set fire to it.'

He looked at her. 'All right. I'll hand it to Benson and get a receipt in your name. We'll keep Connie and Malc out of it.'

He gave a final glance round the room. He wasn't

looking for anything else, but he drew out the drawers of Donna's dressing table. Good quality underwear, neatly ironed, a section for jewellery: earrings, chains, necklaces, not expensive, not tat, a stack of *Hello!* magazines in the bottom drawer, and two paperback novels by Jeffrey Archer.

'She wasn't much of a reader,' Patsy said sadly. 'It was either the telly or her sewing.' She glanced round the sweet-smelling room. 'We'd often sit in here together. We did get on, you know, a lot of the time. She was good company. And so funny, especially about the blokes. And with looking such an innocent, such a good girl … well, you know. And she'd do things for you, she'd see to my clothes as well as her own, that sort of thing. As long as it didn't involve money. Always swore she'd not got a two pence coin to scratch her arse with.'

He riffled through the pages of the Archer books. It was some time later before he knew they meant more to the case than the money ever did.

'I wish it would last and last,' she said, 'the case. Even though it's about poor Donna.'

They were back at Conway House, where Crane was writing up the details of the money they'd found, for Anderson to get tense and frustrated about all over again because he'd not been involved. Crane put down his felt tip, shrugged and said, 'I'm anxious to get it over as soon as possible, to save your people the expense, but I know what you mean. We've had some good evenings, haven't we, round the flip chart, pooling ideas?'

'I've never known anything like it. Seeing you guys in action, the way your minds work. I shan't ever forget it.'

He could believe it. Nothing like this had ever happened to her, something so intriguing and involving, where she'd felt both useful and needed. It was as if she'd come fully to life. There was an impression of assurance in her plain features now, due to the care she was taking of her looks and her clothes. Genuine self-confidence would come later, when she began to progress at work, as he was certain she now would.

'Are you married, Frank? Partner?'

He smiled, shook his head. 'People like me and Anderson find it hard to live a normal life.'

She said, 'Life won't seem the same when you have to go off on some other case and you're not popping in every day.' There was an unmistakeable warmth in her lavender eyes.

'I'll be around, Patsy. I'll always want to know how you're doing.'

When he'd gone, she sat over her drink, hugging herself. There wasn't another woman! He'd promised he'd be around! Could she have a chance with that lovely bloke? She'd not care how hard he worked. She was used to the hours he kept, as she'd worked with him....

Benson put the bag of fifties in a document-case. 'Silly bitch,' he growled. 'Seven grand against staying alive. Right, I'll get them examined and I'll make out the receipt to Patsy.'

He spoke grudgingly, and Crane knew he was exasperated because he'd found something else a police search had missed. He sighed inwardly, what with him and Anderson....

'And you reckon Fletcher's a no-no? We thought so too.'

'Can't be ruled out, I suppose. Blokes lost their tempers around Donna.'

'Could have threatened to dump him. Said he wasn't getting her anywhere. The national agencies have branches in Leeds, after all.'

'My thinking too. And I'm positive he went on somewhere that night.'

'We'll keep up the pressure on him. Two or three days and we should be ready to think of a new start. Who's it going to be, nailing the killer then, assuming anyone does,' Benson said, giving a pained smile. 'You or us?'

'Don't forget that smooth-talking bastard, Anderson. He's not as clever as he likes to think he is, but by God he's focused, and he doesn't regard coming second as an option.'

Crane knew Benson had nothing to lose. Whoever pinned down the killer the police would calmly chalk it up as their own result. That was life.

Leaf and Petal covered two or three acres. There were the usual greenhouses and lines of saplings, together with collections of seasonal flowers, bags of compost, garden furniture and stone ornaments. The walkways were busy with couples pushing their purchases in shallow trollies. The leaves of plants and shrubs were beaded with the drops of a recent watering and glittered in sunlight. They entered the main building, a single-storey complex of linking rooms, filled with lawnmowers, seed packets in stands, displays of weedkiller and fertilizer, and racks of gleaming tools. A fragrant coffee smell drifted from a central snack bar.

'Best not to have him paged,' Anderson said. 'We'll just find him and give him a lovely surprise, yes?'

They found Hellewell in a room of intense humidity. Sun poured through skylights on to a dense and pungent collection of house plants. There was a low murmur of voices and Hellewell was courteously displaying his knowledge of the vagaries of indoor plants to a pair of elderly women who looked as if they were being given rather more information than they really needed. He glanced towards the men with a pleasant smile, which faded when he saw Anderson.

'Well, I hope that answers your question, ladies,' he said, in hasty conclusion. They drifted off, looking vaguely stunned. 'And what do *you* want?' he said, sighing heavily.

'This is Frank Crane, Mr Hellewell,' Anderson said, amicably polite as ever. 'He's a private investigator, working for Donna Jackson's parents. We're acting together.'

'But ... Mahon's the man. I know they can't pin—'

'He's been cleared, sir. The case needs a fresh start.'

He looked very uneasy. It had been a shrewd move of Anderson's to leave them unannounced. He watched them in what seemed like a frightened silence. He was near six foot, fortyish, and in good physical shape, probably because of the outdoor work he did. His fair hair had a slightly bleached look with sunlight exposure. He was tanned, had well-shaped features and white, even teeth. Women could never be too good looking, but some men could. Hellewell, it seemed to Crane, was one of them.

'Why ... why aren't the police here then? Why you two?'

'The police are aiming to make a completely new start shortly.'

He watched them in another edgy silence. He wore a

short-sleeved green shirt and jeans, and the sunlight flooding the room gleamed on the hairs of his muscular brown arms. Sweat looked to be gathering near his hairline.

'I'll wait till the police come then. I've nothing to add to what I said when the poor kid was found, and if you wouldn't mind, this is my busiest time of the year.'

'You'll be doing me and Donna's parents a big favour if we could just talk a little, Mr Hellewell,' Crane said quietly. 'They're very distressed that someone's not facing justice. To be honest, they haven't much money to spend on employing people like me.'

To refuse would seem callous and he knew it. Hellewell sighed again in exasperation. They'd clearly handed him a nasty shock and it was giving Crane a lot more of a buzz than he'd had from Fletcher. There'd always been a puzzle about Hellewell. Was he the J who'd shown in Donna's diary, even sometimes at weekends? If so, being a married man, how had he managed to get away with such a regular affair with an employee?

'You'd better come this way,' he said reluctantly.

They followed him between the crowded plant displays to a tiny corner office. A woman standing near it watched their progress, her eyes on Anderson. She had dark wavy hair and strongly defined looks: thick eyebrows, a straight sharp nose, a full firm mouth. She wore jeans and a white blouse piped in red and bearing the Leaf and Petal logo on the breast pocket.

'*Hello*, Geoff,' she said warmly. 'What brings *you* here? Not to buy any exotics, I'm sure.' She gave him a wide smile that held the sort of warmth Crane had seen in Carol's.

'It's about Donna again,' Hellewell said irritably. 'It seems it's not down to that piece of garbage, Mahon, after all.'

'Oh … shall I sit in?'

'I can't spare you off the floor,' he told her in a curt tone.

'I shall be here if needed, Geoff,' she said pointedly.

'That was Mrs Hellewell,' Anderson told Crane as they went in; it was clear Hellewell wasn't going to bother explaining her. They sat on canvas chairs in the tiny partitioned room, their knees against a self-assembly desk. Hellewell faced them across it.

'We'll make it as brief as possible, sir,' Crane said. 'Just to get things clear in my own mind, would you mind telling us where you were yourself the night Donna went missing?'

'I was with a man called Clement Hebden,' he said shortly. 'I'd finished late on the Saturday and gone to his place with a proposed layout for landscaping his garden. It's a sideline. We got engrossed, had a few Scotches and then I realized I was over the limit. I was going to take a taxi and pick my own up later, but he said why didn't we go on talking and I could sleep in one of the spares. Kirsty was away visiting her mother, so I accepted the offer.'

Crane nodded. Alibis didn't come more bullet-proof than that. 'Thank you, sir. I believe Donna was working here that day?'

'She left at five.'

'Did she form a strong friendship with any of the men she worked with, would you know?'

'No chance.'

'You seem very sure.'

'I am sure. Catch Donna with—' He broke off abruptly.

'What I'm saying is that I *need* to be sure. Staff chat-up can lead to problems and I have to know what's going on.'

But the slight sneer had been there, which had seemed to hint that Donna hadn't wanted to waste her time on men who hadn't got money to spend or favours to grant.

'Just what were her duties, Mr Hellewell?'

He shrugged. 'Same as the others. Took a turn on the checkouts, helped in the café, advised customers about plants and trees.'

'She had a good grasp of nursery work?' Anderson chipped in.

He began to look faintly sheepish. Crane recalled Patsy saying she'd barely known one plant from another. 'Well, she was in learning mode.'

'So she'd just work spring and summer, I suppose, not being one of the skilled staff?'

He coloured very slightly. 'No, she had a permanent position. People do still come, even in winter. And house plants and fir trees at Christmas, we're pulled—'

'But wouldn't your core staff be able to cope with the reduced demand?' Anderson asked, and Crane had to admire his knack for feigned ignorance.

'I can't see what my staff arrangements have to do with anything!' he burst out.

'Perhaps I'm missing something,' Crane said politely, 'but why keep on an unskilled person when there really wouldn't be much for her to do?'

He looked to be biting back another outburst. Then he forced a smile, his first. 'Look, boys, give me a break, the kid looked like a film star, for Christ's sake. She pulled in the punters. She had charm. She'd give the blokes the big dazzling smiles and they kept on coming back here instead of going elsewhere.' His gaze passed between them unfocused. 'I had big ideas for Donna Jackson,' he said, and Crane heard the same catch in his voice he'd heard before in the voices of other men. 'I was aiming to get that Fletcher guy to photograph her in a Leaf and Petal blouse and transpose her image over a view of the nursery. I was going to run it week in, week out in an advert in the *Standard*. I was going to have a big blow up version on a billboard over the main entrance, so that every time you saw that kid's marvellous face you thought of Leaf and Petal.'

'Great idea, Mr Hellewell,' Anderson said with a sympathetic nod.

'Did ... Donna have any other duties, sir, apart from those you mentioned?' Crane spoke hesitantly, as if regretting having to break into Hellewell's mood of sad reverie.

His eyes refocused with an effort. 'She did deliveries. We do those for a few seniors and people who bring a lot of business.'

'Would there be a record of deliveries?'

Crane felt Anderson stirring and could sense his watchfulness. What new ball was the PI running with *now*?

'We keep a book,' Hellewell told them. 'The accounts are drawn up from it as we bill the people we deliver to. The initials of the person who delivers go in the book. What's that got to do with anything?' He looked genuinely puzzled, but Crane guessed Anderson knew.

'I'd just be interested to see where Donna made those deliveries. It might be worth checking out some of the people she made them to. Would you mind letting us see the delivery book?'

Hellewell's wary eyes left Crane's and he keyed a

phone. 'Gail, a man called Mr Crane would like to see the delivery books. It's to do with the audit. He'll be along presently.' He looked back at Crane. 'You'll find her in the checkout area.'

'Thank you. One last point, sir. Do you know of a man Donna might have known called Adrian?'

That was the query that did the business. Hellewell might have had his throat cut the way healthy colour drained rapidly from his face. He shook his head, then shook it again and again. 'I don't know *anyone* Donna knew, apart from Mahon and Clive Fletcher,' he said, through lips he could barely control. 'Any … anyone at all. The name means absolutely nothing to me.'

'Are you sure, Mr Hellewell?' Anderson asked softly. 'You seem a little agitated.'

'It's you lot,' he almost whispered. 'PIs, reporters, police, bombarding me with questions, raking it all up about that lovely kid. I'm sorry, I'm finding it hard to cope.'

It seemed to Crane he'd coped pretty well until he'd heard that single word: Adrian. He knew from experience the value of leaving someone like Hellewell, who clearly knew something and was running scared, to sweat it out for a while. He got up. 'Well, if the name should come back to you in any context, sir, I'd be very glad to know. It's very, very important. Perhaps I could check with you tomorrow?'

'There'd be no point!' he yelped. 'I don't *know* any Adrian.'

'Thank you for your time, sir. Anything else you need to ask Mr Hellewell, Geoff?'

They left him staring into space.

'Brother,' Anderson said, 'did *that* touch the spot. His face changed like a traffic light. That bloody technique of yours, just tossing it in when he thought he was out of the woods. How do you always manage to make it look so easy? And that delivery business, it never crossed my mind. She just might have met someone that way.'

There was a petulance in Anderson's tone that he fought hard to contain. Crane was certain the possibility of Hellewell being linked to an Adrian had to be their hottest lead yet, and should have been the total focus of both their minds, but as usual Anderson was brooding more about Crane's superior skills.

'Geoff,' he said patiently, 'I've been at it for years and I've learnt to let nothing go by default. Checking out deliveries is bound to be a blind alley, but I'll do it anyway. It doesn't begin to compare with him throwing a wobbly about Adrian.'

'You're right,' he said, striving to mask the grudging note. 'OK, this Adrian—'

'Geoff?' Someone spoke from behind them as they made for the checkout area. It was Mrs Hellewell. 'Could I have a word?'

'Of course, Kirsty,' he said, giving her that instant flattering concentration he showed all women. 'This is Frank Crane. We're working together on Donna's case now that Mahon's out of it. He's a private investigator.'

'Hello,' she said absently to Crane. 'I've got my own little cubbyhole off the café. Perhaps we could go in there.'

'Lead the way.'

'It's … well, it's very private. I need your advice.'

'They don't come more discreet than Frank, Kirsty.'

'Please, Geoff. I'm sorry, Mr Crane, no offence.'

'None taken, Mrs Hellewell. I'll go chat to Gail, Geoff.'

Crane watched them walk off. Mrs Hellewell appeared to be looking warily around her. He wasn't happy about this. He couldn't be sure he could trust Anderson not to keep some vital card up his sleeve to put one over on him, in that intense, competitive way he had, and waste him time. Assuming what she had to tell him had any relevance to the case.

Gail was a mousy haired hefty young woman with a cheerful smile. They sat down with the delivery book at a display garden table in the entrance hall.

'You're not the usual auditor, are you?'

'I'm just helping out with the debtor's tab. There are one or two queries that go back to the time when Miss Jackson was here.'

She sighed. 'Poor Donna. She was really, really good on the money side too, making sure everything was invoiced properly.'

He nodded, not needing to be assured of her expert touch on the money side. 'Her initials went against the deliveries she made, yes? So what sort of people did you deliver to?'

'Elderly folk mainly. Wealthy business types short on time. We had to know them really well for Joe – Mr Hellewell – to deliver.'

They began to sift through the names in the months leading up to Donna's death. They all seemed above suspicion, going by Gail's description. 'It was mostly seniors, you see. Some of the business folk did forget to settle their accounts occasionally, that's true. Now then ... Miss Julia Gregson, that was one address she went to several times.' She flicked over pages. 'Funny,' she murmured, 'I remembered thinking at the time what a lot of stuff we sent to Cheyney Hall.'

'Miss Gregson being another elderly lady?'

She shook her head. 'Mid-thirties, I'd say. Pots of brass. Doesn't need to work, I believe. I should be so lucky.'

Instinct told him that this might just be worth checking out, but something more positive prompted him, something he couldn't quite pin down. 'Were all Miss Gregson's deliveries made by Donna?'

She nodded. 'Look, there's a little note here in Joe's writing: "Miss Gregson requests that all her deliveries be made by Donna." That explains it. She had such a nice way with customers.'

'You've been a great help, Gail.' He scribbled down the address of Cheyney Hall. 'I think we've isolated the debt; I'm sure she's just overlooked it. Would you know if Miss Gregson lives alone? No partner?'

'Can't help you there,' she said, grinning. 'Donna never let on. Didn't let on about anything much, to be honest. I should think Miss Gregson's beating them off, with all that lovely dosh, but I only ever saw her here on her own.'

'She's not been in recently?'

She frowned. 'Now there's a funny thing. I don't remember seeing her all season, now you mention it.'

Crane stood near the entrance, waiting for Anderson, though the reporter had his own wheels this afternoon. He was curious about Kirsty Hellewell. Then suddenly, Anderson came careering across the entrance hall, jacket flying about him with the momentum. 'Can't stop, Frank, they've just got me on my mobile. Some nutter in Cutler Heights has a woman and two kids under siege.

Threatening the uniforms with a gun. We'll touch base at Patsy's, OK?'

Crane followed him out, but he went off at an angle. 'My car's in the lower park,' he said. Crane had never seen him so animated and didn't believe it was much to do with a nutter with a gun. Anderson suddenly turned and ran back a few yards, his cocky, triumphant grin an ominous sign. 'I've got fantastic news,' he said in a lowered voice. 'I think we're there, Frank, I think we're there!'

Crane ruefully watched him lope off. It was churlish to feel so disappointed and he knew it. The killer had to be caught and what did it matter who got the lead that counted? But Crane was the pro and he'd wanted it to be him. He got in his car. The reporter had clearly had a stroke of luck. And if he was so charming that women told him things, well, that was part of his luck too. But what could she have told him? Whatever it was, it had to be dynamite.

Anderson drove as rapidly as he dared to join the city ring road. He grinned, the look on Crane's face! He knew this was a ball they could run with. He was almost certain in his own mind that it would solve everything and leave him with a story nearly as good as the original one. Boy, would he be glad when it was all over and he could begin work on the final draft of his big feature, and start to put out feelers to *The Sunday Times*. There was absolutely no doubt in his mind he would eventually get what he wanted. He always had. But the look on Crane's face!

Crane went to Ilkley by the moor road. The sun shone from a clear sky and the rooftops of Ben Rhydding were as sharply defined as an engraving. He drove rapidly, the greeny-brown mass of the moor's terrain rising to his left. He was tense, restless, impatient to know what Anderson had learnt. He had to admit that he was a bright bloke, he'd not be crowing that he thought they were there if he'd not got the strongest lead of all. Crane couldn't shake off his disappointment that a young reporter could get ahead of a police-trained PI. All right, he'd had a massive stroke of luck. It didn't make him feel any better.

He knew this would probably be a pointless journey, but he couldn't settle. He'd decided to see Julia Gregson if only to eliminate someone else who appeared to have got to know Donna rather well, going by the deliveries she'd had her make. That other detail still nagged at his mind, some connection he couldn't quite make.

'Miss Gregson?' he'd asked on the phone.

'Who is this?' she'd said sharply, in the imperious way moneyed people often had.

'The name's Frank Crane. I'm investigating the murder

of Miss Donna Jackson on behalf of her parents. The original suspect has been cleared. Could you spare me a little time if I called on you?'

The silence was so lengthy he thought he'd been cut off. Then, ' I ... fail to see what help I can give you. All she did for me was deliver shrubs and bedding plants.' There was a decided tremor behind the assured hauteur.

'She made an awful lot of deliveries.'

'I've got an extremely large garden.'

'Did you become friends, Miss Gregson?' he said, in a soft tone.

'There's nothing I can help you with, Mr Crane. Goodbye.'

'I'm liaising with the police,' he said quickly. 'I shall have to pass on to them this information, and as they're now on the point of reinvestigating the case themselves I think you'll find they'll insist on talking to you. I could possibly spare you that.'

After another silence, she said in a subdued tone, 'Oh, very well, I'm in all evening.'

The house was off the Ilkley-Skipton road, isolated and standing in extensive grounds, around which ran a high perimeter wall. He drove in through an archway with ornamental gates that stood open. Cheyney Hall was a very grand residence: gabled, chimneyed, stone-built and with a delicately-columned portico sheltering the main entrance. The front garden was mainly sweeping lawn and mature trees, but a central fountain played into a carved stone basin.

She opened the door herself. 'Come in, Mr Crane.'

She led him across a spacious hall, half-panelled and hung with landscapes in oil, and heavy with the scent of freshly cut flowers, which stood in ornate vases. There were more flowers in the lofty reception room she took him into, in more vases standing on carefully polished antique tables: roses, lilies, marguerites, sweet peas and many more he couldn't put names to. It brought to Crane's mind a French tag he'd once read somewhere: *Qui fleurit sa maison fleurit son coeur.*

A phone sounded in a distant corner. She excused herself and left him standing by the window. It was rear facing and the spread of land on this side of the house seemed as vast as a park. It was overlooked by a balustraded terrace and in the foreground the garden was formal and geometrical in the precision of its layout, with a pool that was more like a small lake. Beyond it stretched walkways, tapestried hedges, a gazebo and tiny, separate, secluded gardens, shrouded by cherry, apple and laburnum trees. A distant strip of dense woodland formed a boundary. A lengthy, lavishly stocked conservatory ran from the left of the house at right angles. It was the largest garden Crane had ever seen enclosing a private house. He was so absorbed by the scale of the place that for a few seconds he was unaware of her return. She stood watching him in a wary silence.

'Miss Gregson,' he said politely, 'may I ask why you had all those deliveries made of plants and shrubs you didn't really need?'

She went on watching him in silence. She was about five-six and had dark brown hair looped back into an elegant bun, slightly protruding brown eyes, a rather aquiline nose and an olive complexion. She wore a black rib cardigan and a straight, black, ankle-length skirt. He seemed to detect in her eyes the same bottomless sadness he'd seen several times before in the Donna Jackson case.

'I ... yes ... you're right,' she said heavily at last. 'I ordered many things I didn't need. Would never need. I ... I liked to see her. I grew to care for her. She was so very sweet, such a friendly little thing. That's really all there is to know about Donna and me.'

'You had deliveries made simply to see her for a short time?'

She turned away, absently adjusted an already perfect flower arrangement. 'Well, obviously I'd ask her in for coffee. I live a rather solitary existence. She'd stay and chat for a quarter of an hour. They seemed not to mind at Leaf and Petal.'

'She never talked about boyfriends at all, Miss Gregson? Apart from Mahon, the man the police originally thought responsible for her death?'

For a second, he thought she was going to faint. She closed her eyes, swayed. He caught her arm.

'Are you all right?'

She took several deep breaths, plucked his hand away with a look of distaste. 'She never talked about men. Never.'

'Not even a man called Adrian?'

'She never talked about *men*! She ... she knew ...' She let the sentence dangle.

The outburst abruptly supplied the key Crane hadn't stopped searching for. Her name was Julia and there was a J in Donna's diary he and Patsy had been unable to fit a name to. Crane had assumed it could only be another man. Until now.

'Did you ever see Donna apart from when she made deliveries, Miss Gregson?' he said carefully.

She shook her head, began swallowing. 'Of course not. Why should—'

145

'She didn't come back in the evening now and then? Or at the weekend?'

She shook her head again, but was now swallowing so rapidly she couldn't speak. She burst into tears. He'd seen few women cry as she did. She cried noisily, endlessly, crouching as if in barely endurable physical pain, the tears streaming down her cheeks and dripping off the end of her chin. Few cases he'd known had involved such heart-break. He crossed to a sideboard, poured brandy from a decanter, returned and put it carefully into her shaking hand. She gradually calmed herself, taking sips of the liquor between sobs. She sat on a shield-back chair beside one of the flower-bearing tables.

'You must have guessed what I am,' she said, in a thin, wavering tone.

'You fell for her?'

'She'd come at weekends now and then. I adored her. I begged her to be my secretary-companion. I'd take her all over the world. My father was in property. I couldn't spend what he left me in two lifetimes. But she ... she wasn't as I am. She'd stay with me, even sleep with me, but ...' Her haggard gaze passed over the flawless precision of the formal garden. Crane guessed she'd dressed in black since the discovery of Donna's body. 'We both wept one night because she was, well, she was normal, couldn't commit to ...'

He looked down ruefully at her bowed head. He could have told her that the only reason Donna had wept was because she couldn't hack it permanently with another woman, even if that woman happened to be one of the wealthiest in the West Riding.

'Did you give her money, Julia?'

Her eyes rested on his. 'Not for sleeping with her. Never for that. She'd not have taken it. She was too genuine, too caring. Sleeping together was simply part of our close friendship. But ... yes, I did give her a little money now and then. I'm wealthy, she was poor. The family depended on what she made at the nursery. You'll probably know her father's too ill to work. She'd only ever take money, and so very reluctantly, to help her parents.'

Her eyes began to well with tears once more. It struck Crane then what an incredible inspirer of dreams Donna had proved to be: a companion for Julia, a star model for Fletcher, a billboard queen for Hellewell. She seemed to embody dreams like those legendary actresses who appeared so sensitive, spiritual and pure, and yet, away from the screen, always seemed to live the raciest lives.

'How did it end?' He spoke with deliberate bluntness.

There was a sudden brooding look in her eyes, startling in its intensity. 'I thought it was just me,' she said, in a low raw tone. 'I accepted that we weren't the same, knew she'd have to leave me one day. Some man, children, all that nonsense. All I asked, while we were together, was for it just to be me.' She fell silent for seconds. 'But ... but she *was* seeing someone else. A man. A *man!*' She ended on a note of near-anguish.

'Any idea who the man was?'

Another silence, her gaze unfocused. 'We were ... she was coming to me on Saturday after work. She cancelled, said Joe wanted her to work late, they were so busy. I was very upset. Couldn't quite believe her. I drove to Leaf and Petal and waited in a corner of the car park the staff use. She came out at the usual time, but didn't drive her car, took a taxi. I followed it. It took her to the Raven, out towards Kirby Overblow. He was waiting for her in the car park.'

'What did he look like?'

'I only saw him from a distance, and only from behind. I daren't be seen, I might never have seen Donna again.' Her face looked crumpled in the gathering dusk, as if she'd developed age lines. 'He was fair, well-built, tallish. I took the number of his car when they'd gone inside, then came home. I don't know why I took the number – to challenge her with it, I suppose. I never did, of course.' Her voice had fallen to a whisper.

'Have you still got it?'

'You can have it, for what it's worth.'

It may not be worth spit now. Crane was beginning to feel very uneasy, was beginning to wonder if he'd possibly begun to get ahead of Anderson. She'd been crazy about Donna, like so many others, but it had begun to turn ugly at the point where a man had entered the equation.

'Did you ever visit Tanglewood reservoir with Donna?' he said flatly.

She flushed. 'What can you be thinking?' she said. 'What can you be *thinking*?'

'Well, did you?'

'You can't imagine I had anything to do with—'

'I'm asking if you went to Tanglewood with her.'

Shaking now and agitated, she watched him again in one of her silences, bottom lip caught in teeth. 'She ... once came here by taxi,' she muttered reluctantly. 'Her motor wasn't very reliable. She couldn't stay over, it was mid-week. I drove her home. She didn't want me to see where she lived, not that I'd have minded. We ... we said our goodbyes at Tanglewood. Sitting on a bench near the lower one. Then I dropped her off on the outskirts of, what do they call it, the Willows?' Her eyes brimmed with tears yet again.

'Julia,' he said, still bluntly, 'Donna kept a diary.'

Her mouth fell open, her moist eyes suddenly wide with shock. 'Oh, no,' she whispered. 'Dear God, *no* ...!'

Crane let the silence roll. Then he said, 'She didn't enter names in it or how she spent her time, she just used single initials. The initial J occurs again and again. It gives the impression that up to the day she died she was here every weekend.'

Mouth still open, the pupils of her eyes rimmed in white, she cried, 'But she didn't! She came a lot, perhaps one weekend in three, but not every *week*.'

She spoke with a vehemence that threw Crane. 'I ... think you'll find the police will put the same interpretation on the diary as me, Julia.'

She fell silent yet again, giving an impression of some kind of mental struggle. Finally, she said, 'Wait,' in a voice of intense reluctance. She got up, crossed to a chiffonier, opened a drawer, returned. She held an inch-thick, leather-bound book. 'If you won't believe me ... I kept a diary too.' She held it out, but hesitantly, as if prepared to snatch it back if he tried to take it. 'Look at it, if you must,' she said sighing.

He drew it slowly from her, turned to the Saturday Donna had last been seen alive. 'Donna,' the entry read, 'didn't come today ...

I wanted her to, of course but mustn't be clingy. Have to accept that she does other things, sees that bloody *man*, I suppose. Oh God, how I miss her. Can't stop thinking of when she was here last and we took a picnic basket along to the Wild Garden. She does love flowers so, begs me to fill the house with them, even though she seems not to know one from another. She was wearing a little blue dress and the sun made her hair shine, and she was the loveliest creature I'd ever seen. I spent most of the day helping Norman with the borders. Then I had a solitary dinner and watched an old film. I was in bed for half-ten. Couldn't sleep. Couldn't stop thinking of how she looked, laughing and chatting and sipping Muscadet. And how much I loved her.

Crane said, 'Do you mind if I look back for three months?'

'Only ... only to check out the weekends. As you can imagine, no one was ever intended to see it.'

The diary provided a complete sheet for each day. He flicked back through the pages covering each Saturday and Sunday beneath her watchful gaze, to check the weekends Donna was present. If the diary was accurate, she really had seen her only about once every two or three weeks. In which case, who was the other J Donna had recorded? Hellewell? The entry for the Saturday Donna went missing was the last. He guessed she'd have written that on the Sunday before she'd heard the news.

'I was too distraught to write anything at all when I was told the police were searching for her,' she whispered. 'I've never kept a diary since.'

'Well,' he said, in a gentler tone, 'thank you for your time, Julia. I'm sorry for the distress I've had to cause you.'

She showed him out. 'Can I be allowed to put all this behind me?' she said in an almost pleading tone, as they stood on the marble tiling beneath the front door's portico.

'I'm ... sorry. I'm afraid, your involvement with her was such that the police will have to know about it.'

She gave a fatalistic nod. She knew as well as he did she was now a suspect and would need to be formally eliminated. Assuming she was innocent. Crane knew he was getting mixed vibes. She could have written up a diary that absolved herself some time after the event.

As he turned to go, she said quietly, 'Frank?'

He turned, waited. The light flowing from the hall outlined her sturdy figure. 'Donna ... one night she woke up trembling. She'd had a frightful dream. I sometimes wonder if it was a premonition. She was in a state. Normally she never spoke about her ... other life. She was very discreet. It was something to do with the photography man, the one who wanted her to be a fashion model. In the dream she'd decided he wasn't good enough, hadn't got the connections. She told him she wanted to enrol with a professional agency. He went berserk. Said she'd never work for anyone but him. He'd ... he'd discovered her. He made the most appalling threats. To her looks, to her ...'

'Go on, Julia.'

'She calmed him down, said she hadn't meant it, she'd just been silly. None of it was really as I'm telling you. She was utterly distraught, almost incoherent. It must have been the dream. She was usually so self-possessed. And she was sobbing her heart out, poor darling. Said she didn't *want* to go away with him. Not now. She said he was trying to control her, make her into something she wasn't. She wanted to live her own life. She was certain he'd try to change her ...'

Crane was becoming puzzled. 'This was still the photographer?'

'I don't think so. It was all so very disjointed, but I think it was another man she was talking about then, who wanted her to go away with him. I think it was the man I saw at the Raven.'

'What happened then?'

'I made her a warm drink. When I came back she was her usual self. Made light of it. Even began to giggle. It had just been a bad dream and I'd not to take any notice, she could handle it.'

'Thanks for telling me. You didn't think to pass it on to the police originally?'

'I ... I couldn't face my life with her coming out, perhaps even getting in the papers. I'm a very private person. And it seemed so likely that this man Mahon ...'

He watched her, wondering if she might not have felt an overwhelming sense of relief when no police had come knocking on her own elegant door eight or nine months ago.

Anderson was already at Patsy's, scribbling on the flipchart, on the page devoted to Joe Hellewell, as wound up, it seemed, as Crane himself was. 'Where have you *been*, you bugger, when it's all happening?'

'What about the siege?'

'All over in an hour.' He grinned. 'I told the desk to hold two inches at the bottom of page nine unless something really big had broken like a cat up a tree. The gun was an imitation and he was so gone on skunk I don't think he knew which century it was, let alone day.' He turned to Crane with a look of triumph. 'There's your killer, sunshine.'

'*Hellewell*?'

'Don't bother with the flip chart just yet. Listen to this.' He put a micro-cassette recorder on the table. Crane glanced at Patsy, who shrugged, drawing down her mouth at the corners.

He said, 'Just before you begin, how come you know Kirsty so well?'

'Last summer Leaf and Petal had a lot of saplings destroyed. The police nailed someone from another nursery trying to damage their trade. I went to report on it with a camera man. Hellewell was away on business at the time and I spoke to Kirsty. I think she took a bit of a shine to me.' He smiled with a faux modesty as carefully honed as his charm. 'One of their runabouts is a Scenic and I casually mentioned I fancied one myself. She made me borrow it for a couple of days to see if I liked it. Really nice woman. And then, when Donna's body was found, I was along there again, talking to her and Hellewell and the rest of the staff.'

Crane recalled Carol at the Glass-house, acting a giggle, and asking him had there been any woman involved in the Donna affair who might have caught Anderson's eye. Well, maybe there had been.

Anderson said, 'I asked her if she'd mind if I used this; she said she actually wanted it on record.'

He pressed the PLAY button. They heard Kirsty say, 'I'm very, very worried, Geoff. I should have told the police at the start. He *was* seeing Donna.'

'Joe? We'd thought he might have been.'

'I began to suspect when he wanted to keep her on for that first winter. She was quite useless for any of the real work we do in winter, all the preparation for the new season. It meant we paid her virtually to do nothing. But he wanted to be certain of having her in place the following spring.' She gave a sigh. 'He had a point, she really did seem to pull in the customers. She was a right little charmer. But then he couldn't keep away from her. I knew perfectly well there was something going on. I should have had it out with him, threatened divorce, but … well, we're not simply married, we're married to Leaf and Petal. We have two kids, they're keen to come into it one day.' There was a lengthy pause. 'I should have told the police at the time.'

'Why didn't you, Kirsty?'

'Because I simply couldn't believe it could be him who … he was so *gone* on her. It broke him up when they found the body. I just couldn't believe … Not Adrian.'

'*Adrian*?' Anderson's voice repeated, high with surprise. 'But … but we're talking *Joe* here.'

'Oh, dear, I sometimes forget. His names are Adrian Joseph, but he always felt Joe sounded more friendly with customers and staff. We call him Adrian at home: family, close friends.' She gave a hollow chuckle. 'A bit like the Royal family, official and unofficial names, King George being called Bertie behind the scenes.'

Anderson paused the recorder. 'Adrian, guys!' he cried gleefully. '*Adrian*! The first piece in the jigsaw. But it gets better, a whole lot better. Stay tuned!'

He pressed PLAY again, to the sound of his own voice. 'I *see*. Two different names. Do you think he was Adrian to Donna?'

'Probably. I think he felt it made him two separate people. I was genuinely sorry about Donna, truly, and though he was so dreadfully upset I felt we had a chance to get our own lives on track again, Ade and me, only …'

There was another lengthy silence. 'And then ... and then I found out he was bisexual. I overheard two of the girls talking in one of the greenhouses about a wealthy customer of ours, Clement Hebden. One of them said, "All that lolly and those cool looks, why does he have to be one of them?" It gave me such a shock. I'd no idea he was gay. Adrian spent an awful lot of time with him, but he was supposed to be helping him landscape his garden. But the night Donna went missing Adrian said he'd stayed the same night at Clement's. Said he'd had a drink too many.'

'That's what he told us earlier.'

'I'll spare you the details of how I proved to myself he was ... that way, but I just had to. It had already been too much trying to cope with his affair with Donna, but, well, if there were men involved too ... I knew I couldn't handle it, Geoff. He was making what he thought were secret trips to Tanglewood. I ... got it together. For months now I've been trying to decide the best way to break with him. It was when I read about that poor man called Ollie being almost battered to death that I began to get really, really frightened, because he was just thought to be a harmless gossip. I couldn't help wondering if he'd somehow found out too much. And then I began to wonder if Adrian really had something to do with ... Donna's death, and his gay friends were perhaps ...'

'Covering for him?'

'Yes,' she said flatly. 'And with Bobby Mahon out of it ...'

Anderson flicked off the recorder, almost shaking with excitement. 'You see? You see? She's reached exactly the same conclusion we did, from the *inside!*'

'That really is one clever lady!' Crane forced himself to

look as jubilant as he sounded. 'Well *done*, Geoff! It's all circumstantial, but once the police have a chance to interview them separately, Hellewell and Hebden, they could be home and dry. If Hellewell really is in the frame I reckon Hebden's going to crack about that alibi.'

'Oh, Geoff, I'm so glad!' Patsy said. 'It's going to mean so much to Mam and Dad if they can see an end to it.'

Crane wished he could feel genuinely pleased. He was certain the reporter had got there. And he was equally certain Kirsty Hellewell would never have talked to him as she'd talked to Anderson. Anderson had had an incredible stroke of luck, and though Crane was exasperated with himself he knew he was going to feel upset about the Donna Jackson case whenever it came into his mind, even though all that mattered was nailing the killer. Amateurs, one, pros, nil, he thought bitterly, behind his smile.

'Well,' he said wryly, 'while you were writing up all this gold-plated stuff from Kirsty, I was in Ilkley talking to a Miss Julia Gregson. She's one of the Js in Donna's diary. There seem to be two Js, but I doubt if the second one's relevant.'

He gave them an outline of what he'd been told at Cheyney Hall, writing up the key points on a sheet of the chart he'd set aside for Julia. Anderson became unusually silent as he talked and scribbled, and when he turned back to them he'd begun to go pale with what looked to be barely controllable anger, an anger so powerful he seemed almost to be quivering. But he quickly forced his usual amiable smile and bantering tone, though Crane sensed it was not without considerable effort.

'Christ, Crane, is there *anyone* your equal for turning up jokers?'

'I'm not with you,' he said, genuinely puzzled.

'Well, from where I'm standing it now looks as if the killer could be any one of three.'

'Oh, come on, Gregson's not in the same league as Hellewell. Nor is Fletcher. Why the frustration, you've brought the bacon home? Gregson was genuinely heartbroken and she'd kept what looks to be a genuine diary.'

'They're all heartbroken. And the diary could have been written after the event, as you said yourself. And why didn't she tell the police? She'd been with Donna at Tanglewood, just like Hellewell.'

Crane watched him in a surprised and uncertain silence. The intensely competitive animal that Anderson was still thought he was outclassing him. Only that could explain the barely concealed fury. But his powerful reactions were raising fresh doubts in Crane's own mind. He'd virtually ruled out Julia on hearing the tape, but she'd had a long time to make her story authentic, even if her emotions had to have been totally genuine. But then he saw he was overlooking the crucial aspect of this very complex case. 'Ollie *Stringer!*' he said. 'Don't forget Ollie. I ask him about Adrian and two days later he's lying in a hollow left for dead.'

'Hasn't it occurred to you that Hellewell and Gregson might have colluded, Frank? You say Gregson's sturdy, so she'd have had the strength to see off a small woman like Donna. But what if she was seen the night they sat on the bench? What if one of the gays told Adrian, out of spite? Adrian certainly knew Donna was with Gregson a lot. What if he twigs Gregson did it and puts the bite on her for some of her loot? He'd still have the motivation to duff up Ollie if he thought Ollie was asking too many of the wrong kinds of questions.'

It hadn't occurred to him that Adrian and Julia might be in it together. The cocky, quick-thinking beggar had him there. At one time he'd not have thought a woman like Julia Gregson could possibly have been involved in such a scene, but having been in the police he'd quickly come to accept that almost anyone could be involved in almost any bloody thing.

'Good thinking, Anderson,' he said, trying for the other's affable manner with the same limited success. He believed he had it sussed now, why the reporter had been so incensed. He'd had his ace trumped with what Crane had uncovered at Cheyney Hall. Instead of winning the race he had merely dead-heated.

'Well, why aren't you jumping up and down, you two?' Patsy asked, in amazement. 'With all the new things you've found out between you?'

Crane knew it was because they were both too evenly matched, both very, very touchy about their skills, and were in a situation that was like one of those games of chess where it seemed that neither player was going to win.

Crane saw Benson in the Toll Gate. He gave him a rundown of everything he and Anderson had found out. Earlier, he'd phoned him with the vehicle number Julia Gregson had taken from the car at the Raven restaurant. The National Computer had shown it as registered to Leaf and Petal.

'And the description she gave roughly matches Joe, slash, Adrian Hellewell,' Crane told him, 'but it could mean she has her own devious reasons for wanting him in the frame.'

'It's not looking good for either of them. She knows bloody well she should have come forward.' Benson stubbed out his second cigarette, then added, with obvious reluctance, 'Good work, Frank. Terry's going to be pleased.'

When they'd both been in the force, best mates, frequently working together, Benson had never really been aware by how much Crane had outclassed him, as Crane, out of friendship, had always encouraged the impression that their decisions had been taken jointly. When Crane had left he knew that Benson had then been forced to accept himself at his true value. And hadn't much liked it.

'Anderson had *the* breakthrough.' Crane tried to sound gracious. 'He had luck; Kirsty fancies him rotten. It did him no end of good when it came to soul-baring time.'

'I knew the bugger would go far.'

'What's the form now?'

'I'm going to Leaf and Petal this afternoon with a DC, get Hellewell and the shirt lifter in for questioning. I'll be in touch....'

Crane got on with routine work with a routine feeling of flatness that a challenging case might soon be out of his hands, bar the tying up of loose ends. But in the early evening things suddenly began to happen.

'Ted here, Frank. Hellewell's legged it.'

'Go on.'

'Kirsty says he worked over alone at Leaf and Petal last night. Someone picked him up, she doesn't know who. Left his own car.'

'Hebden?'

'No, he's been in London since yesterday lunchtime. It checks out.'

'What does Kirsty think?'

'That he's somehow caught on she's grassed him to Anderson. She's not keen to see him back if he thinks she knows too much as well. I've left the DC with her, just in case.'

'What gives now?'

'We start searching. We'll find him sooner or later, God knows what it'll take in man hours. If the fairies have him squat it could take weeks.'

Crane's mobile rang again the second he'd cleared it. 'Oh, Frank, I'm so glad I got through,' Patsy gasped. 'I've been broken into! When I got home from work the door was ajar and the lock smashed.'

'I'm on my way. You've told the police?'

'Before I rang you.'

'Much missing?'

'That's the trouble, nothing I can see. They've not taken the telly or the DVD-player and my few bits of jewellery aren't worth nicking.'

This made Crane uneasy. When he got to the flat she was sipping from a mug of tea, hands trembling. 'Am I glad to see you?'

He took out his mobile. 'I'll get someone to fit a new lock. We can sort it with the insurers in the morning.' He gave details to a locksmith contact. 'You're *sure* nothing's been taken?'

'Nothing. I've looked everywhere. I had a few tenners in a tea caddy. Still there. What can it mean, Frank?'

'I don't know.' He glanced around the living room. Everything looked exactly as it had looked on those other nights, when they'd been gathered around the flip chart. The flip chart itself was neatly closed, as if the intruder had also lacked curiosity, as well as the wish to steal any of her modest possessions.

'I'll get you a drink,' she said.

Preoccupied as he was, he realized there was something different about her. She was wearing a sage green jacket, a short pencil skirt and a black top and even more care than usual seemed to have been taken with her appearance. 'You're looking posh again,' he said, 'as your dad would say.'

'I've been promoted. Officially. I'm a supervisor from the first of next month.'

'Well, that's great! Just great.' He put his hands on her shoulders and kissed her cheek. He wished it hadn't made her lavender eyes shine quite so warmly.

'I could have done without a break-in on a day like this. I was hoping I could take you for a meal, with the case looking as if it's nearly over.'

'You're right, the bastard's timing couldn't be worse.'

'I don't suppose we could go out? When the lock man's been? This is just vandalism. You know what kids on the estate are like.'

He would genuinely have liked to go for a meal. He knew he'd have to steer a careful line between his friendship for her and her attraction to him, but he'd have enjoyed talking about her promotion. It would have pleased him to encourage her to look even further ahead. Complete her education, learn computer skills. He knew now she was the type who could do things, all she'd ever needed was encouragement.

'Sorry, Patsy, but the break-in bugs me, don't ask me why. We'll go out somewhere soon, I promise.' She began to look as uneasy as he felt. 'Don't worry,' he told her, patting her arm, 'I'll sort it.'

He looked around the room again. He'd have felt easier if it *had* been vandals, nicking her telly and her tea-caddy money, trashing the room, scribbling on the pages of the flip chart. The *flip chart*!

'Patsy, was it you who closed up the flip chart last night?'

She gave him a puzzled look, slowly shook her head. 'I always leave it exactly as you and Geoff leave it.'

'Well, I went after Geoff last night and I left it open on the last sheet. The one I did on Julia Gregson.'

'I don't understand.'

'What if whoever broke in was only interested in the flip chart itself?' He was already keying his mobile. 'Geoff? Frank. Look, Geoff, two things. Hellewell's legged it and Patsy's been broken into.'

'Keep talking.'

'Nothing's been taken from the flat, but I'm pretty sure the flip chart's been tampered with.'

'Who'd want to do that? Who'd even know about it?'

'You don't think it could be Hellewell? One of his pals?'

Anderson was silent for a couple of seconds. 'Do you realize what you're saying, Frank? God, all our thinking, all our notes. They'd give him the full picture. He'll know he's the leading suspect!'

'That could be why he legged it. Kirsty told Benson he was picked up. Someone must be helping him.'

'Frank,' he said slowly, as if to calm himself, 'we've got to apply some rigorous analysis here before we get too carried away. How could Hellewell know about the flip chart?'

'Could you possibly have been followed yesterday, from Leaf and Petal?'

'It's ... possible, I suppose. But I went on to the siege.'

'Maybe he tailed you there and then on to Patsy's.'

'Still possible. He'd have gone unnoticed in the crowd.'

'Look, you talked to Kirsty in her own office. Maybe Hellewell found out and wondered what she could be telling you. He must have known things weren't the same between them any more. Let's say he feels he's got to know, shadow's you to Patsy's place, but maybe thinks it's *your* place. He could have sneaked in behind you to pin down the actual flat, the front door takes several seconds to close and lock itself.'

'You know, I think someone *did* come in behind me when the lock was tripped. I thought nothing of it, people are always in and out.'

'Once he knew the exact flat, maybe he decides to come back when he thinks you'll be out and go through your notes, tapes, whatever he can lay hands on. So then he drives back to the garden centre and pretends to be working late. He could have nipped back this morning, after checking you were at the *Standard* office and most of the other residents would be at work. A credit card would open the front door, it's a simple mechanism.'

'If that's how it did happen he certainly hit the jackpot!'

Crane smiled sourly. The flip chart had been the whiz kid's idea, not his. 'Well, if it *is* Hellewell, and I can't see who else it can be, all he's doing is digging himself in deeper. And why leg it if you've got a clear conscience?'

'It would be handy if we could nail him ahead of the police.' The excitement was rising in his voice again. 'The A Team!'

'And make a proper job of it.' Anderson's enthusiasm was catching.

'I'm working out of town just now, but I'll be in touch as soon as I'm back. He'll not go far without money and help. Good luck, pal.'

Crane knew he didn't mean those final words, but it was a nice gesture. Patsy's troubled eyes met his. He said, 'You'll have got most of that, yes? We can only see it being Hellewell, and now it looks as if he might know everything we know. But I'm certain it doesn't affect you, so you mustn't worry. Me and the paper boy are determined to sort it.'

He rang Hellewell's home number. Kirsty answered

quickly, sounding very nervous. 'Mrs Hellewell? Frank Crane. I was with Geoff yesterday.'

'What is it, Mr Crane?'

'Geoff played me the tape he made with you. We're working together, as you know.'

'That's all right,' she said in a low voice. 'It was only because I know Geoff so well, and not knowing you ...'

'I quite understand. It's vital your husband's found, Kirsty, if only so he can be eliminated from the new investigation. You told DS Benson that Joe was working late, but would you know if he was away from the nursery some time in the early evening? For about an hour or so?'

'I really couldn't tell you. I came home not long after Geoff left.'

'Would any of the staff know, do you suppose?'

'I doubt it. Joe's always here, there and everywhere. It's the nature of the job.'

'All right. Would you know if he took his passport with him?'

'Let me look, I keep them all together. You can go on talking, I'm using a cordless.'

'You think he was picked up?'

'We have CCTV now. The police asked me to check the tape. A car drew up near one of the greenhouses about nine. It was too far from the cameras to see the number or who was in it, though the police have ways of sharpening the picture. It could be a Honda ... maybe an Accord.' As she talked, Crane could here the sounds of drawers being opened. 'Ah, his passport's still here.'

'Good, it narrows the field. Thanks a lot, Kirsty, you've been very helpful.'

She was silent for a short time. 'Mr Crane, Frank ... do

you think there's any possibility, any at all, that Adrian …
Joe, didn't do for that poor kid?' she said quietly. 'I'll never
live with him again, but we've been together a long time
and we have a family. We were very happy once, when we
were building the business up. I'd give anything to know
he wasn't involved.'

'Anything's possible, Kirsty,' he said gently. 'And so the
sooner we find him the better.'

'But you think it was him, don't you? You and Geoff?'

There was no answer to that, at least not one that held
the smallest crumb for her comfort.

He cleared his mobile. Patsy was standing before the
flip chart, reading the last completed sheet. She sighed. 'I
feel sorry for Julia. She must have been in an awful state to
break down the way you said she did. She must have been
crazy about Donna. I can see it all. No one could play the
sweet little innocent like Donna. I always had an idea she
attracted both sides. I wonder who the other J could be.'

Crane shrugged. 'I don't think it matters any more.
Another married bloke, maybe, just keen to keep his head
down.'

'I wonder if Donna let anything slip about anyone else,'
she said, in a musing tone. 'I know she was secretive, but
two women together, pillow talk, all that. Something Julia
might have written in her diary, seeing as she kept a
proper one. It might help put Hellewell away, mightn't it?'

'Julia wouldn't have wanted to know, Patsy. She hated
hearing about Donna and men. I'm sure the bad dream
was an exception. And if—' He broke off abruptly, stood
staring at the flip chart. 'Christ, maybe you're ahead of
both me *and* Geoff.'

'How do you mean?'

'If Hellewell's seen the flip chart he knows about the diary too, knows about Donna's affair with Julia. What if he had the same idea as you and thinks the diary could implicate him? He might think Donna really did let his name slip at some point, that there might even be a mention somewhere that she was seeing him the Saturday she died.'

She paled, watched him a little open-mouthed, not quite understanding. 'Look, Patsy, let's say he saw off Ollie, or tried to, because he found out Ollie had been talking to me. So what if he's aiming to do the same to Julia and then destroy the diary? He doesn't know she took the number of his car that night at the Raven, because I wasn't going to put it on the chart till Benson had checked it out. In other words, he just thinks Julia saw someone at the Raven who *might* have been him. But if she's out of it and he and Hebden stick to the story he was with him the night Donna disappeared, well, he could decide the evidence is too flimsy to do him any real harm.'

'But … what if Hellewell and Julia really were in it together, like Geoff thought they might be?'

'Geoff had a good point. So what if Julia had killed Donna, and Hellewell thinks if she's taken in for questioning he might be fingered for colluding with her? That's a very serious offence in a murder. He'd go inside, his business and reputation could be ruined. But if Julia could be made to disappear …' He paced up and down the little room. 'I think I'd better go over there. Warn her to be on her guard. Whether she's in the frame or not it's essential the police get her in one piece. I'm really worried now, Patsy, she's isolated and she lives alone and I'm pretty sure the staff only come in the daytime. I've got to go. I'll call in on the way back. The locksmith should be here any minute.'

It was dark now after a day of low cloud. He drove to Ilkley on the quicker route this time, along the valley road, through Guisely and Burley and then along past the silently flowing Wharfe. When he reached Cheyney Hall he pulled up on to the verge, took out his mobile, keyed her number. She'd not want to open the door without knowing who was going to be out there. When he got through, there were odd grating sounds, as if the phone were being picked up uncertainly. There was a brief, breathy silence and then words that came out almost as a sob. 'Help me …'

'Julia? What's the—'

Then she screamed. A scream that seemed curtailed. It made the hairs on his neck prickle. He heard a dull sound that could have been a blow, followed by a crashing noise that had to be the fall of a body. The connection was carefully broken.

E L E V E N

Crane scrambled out of his car and ran towards the arched entrance. The gates stood open as before. There was a car on the drive, just within the gates. He'd grabbed a torch on leaving the Megane. Its glow identified the car as a Honda. An Accord. His heart lurched. He ran on to the great front door. It was locked. He moved cautiously to the right, as it was so dark, and round to the back of the house to where the wide terrace overlooked the vast rear garden. He had to locate the room that had been filled with flowers.

She lay on an oriental rug before an ornate fireplace. The room was dimly lit by a single table lamp, but it looked to have been overturned in a struggle, so that its light was concentrated on her body in its black clothes, and left the man's features in shade. But he caught a glint of fair hair and the outline of a strong frame and he knew it was Hellewell. He tried the handle of the french window. It gave. Perhaps she'd been out on the terrace earlier. That must have been how he'd got in.

As the french window opened, with a faint whine, Hellewell fled through a door that Crane knew would take him into the big hall. Crane dropped to his knees at Julia's side. She'd been given a blow with some object, possibly an ornament, and the wound extended from her left temple into her hair, which was matting with blood. She was breathing, but unconscious. He heard noises in other parts of the house. Was Hellewell trying to get out? And finding the doors deadlocked?

There was an antique chest of drawers on cabriole legs to the left of the door. It was heavy but not too heavy to drag in front of the door and block his return. Crane needed to do two things urgently: disable Hellewell's car and get help. It wouldn't be too long before Hellewell found a way out of the house, even if he had to break windows.

Crane went out to the terrace, then returned along it as rapidly as he dared in the pitch darkness. He'd seized a heavy silver candlestick from the fireplace mantel and now smashed in the headlamps and taillights of the Accord. He'd not get far without lights. He then took out his mobile and began to key 999. Hellewell appeared from nowhere, snatched the phone from his hand and flung it in the basin of the fountain. As Crane began to turn, a very hard fist struck his cheekbone in a glancing blow.

He began to run. He was a strong man and tall, but he knew Hellewell would have the edge over him, working daily on his land. He'd had one glancing blow from a fist that felt like granite, if he took a full-on blow coming out of nowhere in this darkness it could disable him. At least he still had his torch and he made his way along the side of the house and round to the terrace again, then ran down the wide steps and on to the path that skirted the pool and led into the formal garden. He'd rarely known such darkness as that which enveloped Julia Gregson's immense property, standing as it did in the lee of unlit moorland terrain.

Beyond the formal garden the land was broken, as he remembered it, by smaller gardens, the gazebo, lofty hedges, pleached archways. Beyond all this again was the boundary copse. Maybe he could make for that, then scale the perimeter wall? He moved as rapidly as he dared, with short bursts on the torch to light his route along one of the main walkways. It seemed to take for ever, but he finally reached a strip of open, well-cut lawn. He was able to race across this, as the land was even, and to reach, with a sigh of relief, the dense forest trees of the copse. He moved warily into an even denser darkness, feeling his way past the massive trunks of the ancient trees, not daring to use his torch now in case Hellewell had somehow caught up with him and spotted the brief flashes of the torch's glow.

But he knew he was becoming disoriented as he picked his way along, with many slight changes of direction. He wondered where Hellewell was. He'd not given instant chase and Crane had heard no sounds at all of pursuit as he'd made his way the entire length of the garden. It made him very uneasy. Had he done a runner? But his car now had no lights. Would he risk using it? Maybe he'd gone off on foot. He didn't want to think he might have gone back inside the house to finish the job he'd come for.

Crane's plan was to scale the perimeter wall and double back to his own car, where it stood on the roadside verge, and ring for help from the car phone. But what if Hellewell had worked that out for himself, and was crouched nearby waiting for his return? It wasn't possible to even guess how his mind would work. He put a hand to his throbbing cheekbone and muttered, 'Christ, Anderson, where are you when I *really* need help?'

And then, glancing behind him, he saw it. It was like the brief flickering of a single star in the vacuum of darkness. It had to be a torch. That must have been what had delayed Hellewell, getting it from the Accord and inspecting the damage to his car's lights. At a guess, the torch had given its single burst from beyond the strip of lawn that separated the garden proper from the copse. Within seconds he'd be in the copse too. He must have plotted Crane's course by the small amount of noise he'd made, the brief flashes he'd had to give on his own torch. He wondered if he should stay completely still. It was difficult to move silently when he couldn't see anything. And attempting to climb the wall would have its own problems. It would be virtually impossible to manage it without giving his position away. Something fluttered to his left, as if a springy branch had been pushed aside and not released carefully enough. It sounded to be several yards away. Crane was worried now that if Hellewell had got a torch from his car he might also have picked up some weapon that could do even more damage than those stony fists of his.

He thought hard. He'd been roughly reoriented by the flash of the other man's torch. He could detect the smallest glow of light coming from the strip of open lawn compared to the near impenetrable conditions in the copse. He decided to make for it, take a chance that Hellewell was aiming to nail him trying to get over the wall. It could keep him occupied for five or ten minutes. Crane was certain he'd know there was a wall there, he must have made deliveries to Cheyney Hall himself in the early days of his business. If he retraced his steps, he might be able to regain the house and ring for help from there.

It wasn't possible to move around without being heard in the total eerie silence of the little wood. Hellewell moved along very slowly and carefully, but the occasional rustle of leaves, the soft crack of a twig underfoot, indicated his progress. Crane decided the stealthy noise of the other man's passage might mask his own movements, and as Hellewell crept in what seemed to be the direction of the wall, Crane inched the other way, towards the strip of lawn. He came to a complete stop every few seconds to ensure Hellewell's progress was still covering the sound of his. Maybe he should have made even more stops. When he halted at the edge of the copse there was a prolonged and ominous silence. And then Hellewell's torch came on and the copse was suddenly filled with crashing sounds as he charged towards the point where Crane had been standing. But Crane was already sprinting across the lawn.

Shapes seemed marginally clearer after the pothole darkness of the copse. Crane ran diagonally to the right, the opposite side of the garden to the way he'd come. From memory again, it had seemed to offer more secluded areas where he could hide while trying to plot his next move. He came to another shade of darkness which appeared to be a tall hedge. He began rapidly feeling his way along it. It was on a curve and he remembered then. There'd been a tall yew hedge that had seemed to form a complete circle. He'd seen one entrance when he'd looked from Julia's drawing room last evening. He reckoned there'd be others. He was right. He came to an opening shortly afterwards and slipped inside the circle, glancing warily behind him as he did. No torchlight, only the profound silence of before.

Then another shock. There were people in the garden, standing motionless. He could almost sense them rather than see them. He shivered, as if he'd fled from one indefinable menace to another. He risked a fast burst on his torch. They weren't people but topiary chessmen. His beam caught a mitred bishop and beyond it a king. It did nothing to stop him shivering. He felt at another of the shapes and decided it must be a castle, an elaborate turreted affair. He crouched behind it and listened, but could hear nothing.

What could Hellewell be aiming to do? Crane was certain he'd have killed Julia had he not been disturbed, just as he'd feared. Killed her, destroyed the diary, got another 'friend' to alibi him for the nights he was missing. But didn't he realize DNA samples might tie him to the scene? It needed only a single hair, a minute flake of the skin everyone shed all the time? Perhaps he'd decided it was worth the risk. If Julia was out of it and there was no diary to tie him to Donna that night at the Raven, he might have decided the police wouldn't have a case. Perhaps he'd been going to make it look as if Julia had surprised an intruder, keen to get his hands on costly antique ornaments, and had been attacked and killed. Perhaps, perhaps....

But Crane had surprised him, and he had to have decided that whoever Crane was he couldn't let him live either. That had to be the logical conclusion. He wished to God he could see. This great garden had become the loneliest and scariest spot on earth. If he could see properly he could at least put up a fight, and might even have a chance of winning. If he was fighting for his life he'd have to.

Where was he now? He still couldn't stop shivering. This area of dark shapes in a dark place was spooking him like a nightmare. He couldn't stop anticipating the oblivion that would go with a savage blow over the head from some tool. Or the appalling, gasping pain of a knife in the back.

Suddenly he knew Hellewell was there. With him in the topiary garden. His eyes were operating at their optimum capacity, and perhaps fear gave them a slightly keener edge. The shapes loomed about him like ghosts, one shade of black on another. But one of those motionless figures had a face with the faintest pallor.

He wondered if the openings in the yew hedge were at compass points, to match the precision of the overall layout. If he rejoined the footpath, which he'd left to crouch behind the chess castle, would it lead him to an opening exactly opposite where he'd come in? He got to his feet and began moving again, as quietly as he could and hunched like an animal.

He'd guessed right. The path led him to an exit from the circular garden. He kept on through it, knowing the small sounds he'd made had to have been amplified in the silent, deathly stillness. And then he heard it again, that sudden heart-stopping rush of thudding feet. And then an even more hideous noise. The crashing sound of blows. Hellewell had to be beating at the chess figures with some weapon, lashing out blindly in every direction in the hope one of those blows would connect with Crane's skull or shatter an arm.

Crane's stomach felt like a bag of crushed ice. He'd no

idea where the opening had led him, but as the sound of the blows receded he risked another burst on his torch. He was now on a broad walkway, where closely planted cherry trees were pleached almost to form a tunnel. Statues on plinths stood every two yards or so along the right, of the naked goddess type, with flowing hair and hands that gracefully protected modesty. The beating sounds behind him abruptly ceased and he leapt behind the third statue in a darkness as impenetrable as that in the copse.

There was a sudden brief burst of torchlight. Hellewell too would need to know where he was. The tunnel of pleached trees would look deserted with Crane hidden; would he keep on going to whatever lay at the end? There was a lengthy silence, lengthy even though the seconds seemed like minutes to Crane's taut nerves. Then came a sudden appalling crash. He felt the ground vibrate slightly through his hands and knees, where he crouched behind the stone goddess. He felt almost nauseous with tension. Hellewell had toppled the first of the statues, which must be free-standing on their plinths. He knew then what his game was. Dislodging the statues gave him two chances. One of them either landed on Crane or badly injured him, or it flushed him out so that Hellewell could then get going with the weapon he had.

There was a second thunderous crash as the next statue went over. He would now be creeping towards the one that sheltered Crane. Crane got slowly to his feet and waited, beads of sweat trickling steadily down his back. He knew only too well that if he waited too long it would be as bad as not waiting long enough. The timing was utterly crucial. The nerve-shredding seconds fell away and he knew Hellewell must now be very close. He could just detect the tiniest movement of his feet on the earth track. Crane breathed slowly and deeply then suddenly toppled his own statue outwards.

'*Christ!*' The whisper sounded almost like a shout. Crane couldn't begin to guess what damage its fall had done to the man, but its descent to the ground had definitely seemed obstructed, so it must have given him some kind of blow on its way down.

He didn't stay to find out. As Hellewell cursed and groaned behind him, he ran to the end of the lengthy tree-tunnel, along the beam of his torch.

The tunnel led to the main conservatory, the one that angled from the left side of the rear of the house. This meant Crane was back in the area of the pool and the formal garden. And at this point there was an opening from the tunnel that provided an escape route.

But he hesitated. He could make a dash for it, possibly even reach his car. But he didn't know what state Hellewell was in. He didn't sound to be out of action, as he'd hoped. His powerful hands must have been reaching for the statue even as Crane began to topple it over. The damage could have been relatively light, maybe a bruised shoulder or a damaged arm. He was no longer making any noise.

Crane tried the door of the conservatory. It wasn't locked, but controlled by a closing mechanism to ensure it wasn't left open by mistake. The door to the house though, at the far end, was sure to be locked. He was certain Hellewell wouldn't believe he'd go in the conservatory. He'd think he'd now be making for his car, by some circuitous route. He crept in, glad that hinges had been kept well oiled. Maybe he could sit it out in here until he was sure Hellewell had gone off into the great rambling spread of land beyond the pool and the formal garden, then pick his time to make for his car and phone. He daren't risk his torch again, but to the right of the door he located what seemed to be a rough wooden table against which leant garden tools. With a sigh of relief, he grasped something with a shaft and handle that had to be a spade or a fork. He was armed. But in seizing it he dislodged some other implement. It began a sliding fall then crashed on to what must have been a concrete floor. Hellewell's torch instantly ignited from halfway along the tree-tunnel and he began to run towards the conservatory. Bent double, Crane scuttled along one of the narrow paths that cut its way past pulpy exotics, oppressively scented flowers and fronds of greenery that touched his forehead like moist hands. He crouched behind a dense screen of foliage towards the centre of the house of glass. He heard the clatter of what could only be the garden tools being swept aside, and then the grating sound of what seemed to be the table itself being dragged somewhere. He cursed. He'd be putting it in front of the door. He grunted with pain as he did so, but the statue clearly hadn't done him any damage he couldn't handle.

The table wouldn't stop Crane getting out, but it would slow him down, give Hellewell enough time, wherever he was in the conservatory, to get to him. Hellewell began thrashing about him now, at plants and foliage and the curtains of dangling fronds. He no longer bothered to douse the torch, as he had Crane cornered. All Crane could see of him was his shape behind a narrow but high-powered beam, and what looked to be a thick heavy stick.

From what he could gather, a path ran down each side
of the wide chamber, with cross-paths to give access to
fixtures laden with plants, flowers and shrubs. Hellewell
wasn't advancing in a straight line, but branching off
along the cross-paths to give his lethal attention to every
square foot of the room, as systematically as a beater
driving game until it broke for cover.

But Crane wondered what break he could possibly
make. Sweat now ran down his spine in rivulets from the
heat needed for the many rare tropical blooms. His mind
seemed almost to seize up with the overwhelming
pungency of the scents clotting the atmosphere. At least he
had the spade. And he was in good physical shape. But not
in Hellewell's class, the action man who spent his entire
life outdoors working the land.

The beating and slashing was getting relentlessly closer.
He forced himself to think calmly and logically. He
pictured the garden again as he'd seen it last evening. His
mind had been trained to gather detail. He recalled the
look of this lengthy conservatory, jutting from the end of
the house, like a pier. Had there been a second entrance
along the side, one that could be reached more easily from
the terrace or the pool area? He was near certain there had
been a glass-panelled door that had barely defined itself
against the glass walls.

Hellewell was about two yards off, working his way
steadily along a cross-path, slashing and clubbing at costly
blossoms and alien wide-leaved plants, even swinging at
hanging flower baskets in case Crane had pulled himself
up on to a beam. Crane estimated he was about halfway
down the lengthy annexe, possibly roughly in line with
the side door. He began to creep to his right behind the

screen of foliage. For part of a second the beam of Hellewell's torch flicked over the conservatory's garden side, but it was enough for Crane to glimpse the door he'd been near-certain would be there. He crept rapidly up to it, holding carefully on to his spade, paused until the torch beam was focused elsewhere, then slipped through the side door and began to run as rapidly as he dared, giving brief flashes on his torch to light his way. But it was no good. Hellewell had razor-edge reflexes to go with the honed body. Within seconds, Crane heard the soft thud of his feet behind him. They were on the circle of lawn now that bordered the pool, which he could see clearly in the light of Hellewell's torch.

Crane was fast, Hellewell was faster. He came up on him so rapidly Crane knew he'd have to protect himself with his spade. He'd need to hold it in both hands to get his full strength behind the blow, so he stuffed his torch in his pocket, swung round and brought the spade down towards the shadowy figure behind the streak of light.

Hellewell dodged the blow with an almost contemptuous agility, and with his beam now locked on to Crane's legs, gave him a blow to the side of his left knee. It sent him sprawling, gasping with pain. He knew, in a nanosecond that this was it. There was nowhere else to go. The torch's beam then trawled with a deliberate, almost sadistic precision over his body. When it reached his head he knew the carefully positioned strokes would follow it. He also knew he'd not be left holding on to life like Ollie Stringer. Not by a single thread.

But suddenly, inexplicably, the area was flooded with light. High-voltage security lamps blazed from points along the house's façade and the balustraded terrace. Both men were momentarily blinded. Except that, when they could see again, Crane wasn't looking at Hellewell, though the man was tall and fair and fit-looking.

'… Geoff?'

'… Frank?'

'Are you all right, Frank?' a voice cried.

It was Julia. She stood on the terrace, looking down at them from across the balustrade, her face pale as wax, her hair dishevelled, the gleaming, bloody patch on her temple clearly visible. She had what looked to be a double-barrelled hunting gun trained on Anderson.

'More or less, Julia,' Crane said, getting shakily to his feet. The pain in his knee was excruciating and he could stand only by taking the bulk of his weight on his right leg.

'Have you any idea what's going on here? Why did that *maniac* attack me? It was you who rang just before he did, I take it?'

He tried desperately to clear a brain that had had one shock too many. 'I ... I rang you from the road outside. I needed to warn you you might be in some kind of danger.'

'From him?'

'No. Someone else. I'm sorry, I'm as much in the dark as you.'

'Frank,' Anderson murmured, 'I'd no *idea* it was you. Thought it must have been one of her retainers.' Incredibly, he was smiling his usual engaging smile.

'But you'd have killed me!' Crane shouted.

'You, whoever you are. Explain yourself,' Julia called, in the peremptory tone Crane knew well. 'The police will need facts that make sense when I ring them.'

'His name's Geoff Anderson, Julia. He's a reporter with the *Standard*. He was supposed to be helping me find Donna's killer.'

She had a haunted look then in the glare of the lamps, some of which, embedded in the border of lawn, threw light upwards. 'Very well, Geoff Anderson, spit it out.'

He went on smiling, with the self-possession Crane had rarely known him lose. But he knew that fast brain would be thinking hard.

'Frank, can you make any kind of guess about what made him *do* this? If you were working with …'

His brain still reeled with the pain in his knee, the throbbing cheek bone, and this final inexplicable shock.

'Geoff, explain yourself. It'll come out in the end anyway. Why did you attack Julia?'

Anderson smiled on in the glare. He'd understand the law; maybe he'd decided that silence was his wisest move at this stage. But there seemed more to it somehow. He almost looked to be relishing the tight spot he was in, to be getting off on the challenge of finding a way out of it.

'Julia, you're sure you've not see him before?'

'No.' She put the hand that had steadied the gun-barrel up to her head, which Crane guessed must be giving her the sort of pain that made thinking difficult. She was one tough woman, even so. 'But he reminds me vaguely of someone I may have seen at some time or other.'

'Try to remember,' he said urgently.

Anderson looked on, as if barely interested. They stood

for some time without speaking in the *son et lumière* brilliance. Showing every sign of considerable effort, she finally broke the silence. 'I … told you about the man I saw with Donna at the Raven. This … Anderson has a look of him.'

Crane glanced back at Anderson. No reaction. It was surreal. What could possibly be the motive for such bizarre behaviour? Was he mentally ill? Surely not.

'There's a bit of a resemblance between Anderson and Joe Hellewell,' he told her. 'Same colour hair, roughly the same height and build. And we're virtually certain Hellewell killed Donna. He'd been seeing her. We also believe he knew about your friendship with her. *I* thought you could be in danger because he'd decided Donna might have told you she was seeing him around the time she disappeared.'

Another lengthy silence as she came to terms with this baffling new information. Then she said slowly, 'But … but it wasn't Joe Hellewell who attacked me, it was this Anderson. So why shouldn't Anderson be the man who killed Donna and was afraid of what Donna might have told me about *him*?' She spoke like a child who drew a simple, innocent conclusion, unaware of the complexities that lay behind the situation.

'He never actually knew Donna, Julia. His only involvement with her began when she was already dead and he was writing his crime reports. He's spent a great deal of his own time these last months trying to get to the truth behind her killing. There's got to be some other reason why he attacked you.'

He looked at Anderson. 'Geoff, I'm doing everything I can to help you here—'

'How do you *know* he never knew her?' Julia cut in doggedly.

Crane watched her. Well, how did he know? He wished he could think more clearly through the fog of pain. He supposed he knew because he trusted what Anderson had told him. He'd seen her around, you couldn't miss her if you trawled the city's night scene. But he'd never known her.

Or said he hadn't.

A cold hand seemed to touch the nape of his neck. It couldn't be, it couldn't! He'd worked with Anderson, seen the dedication, the drive, the obsessive determination to see a killer nailed. He was trusted by everyone, none more than Connie and Malc for the kindness and sympathy he'd shown them in their distress. Could Anderson himself be somehow involved in Donna's death? It was too ridiculous. And yet ... why had Julia been so viciously attacked? Two or three more blows like the one she'd had and she could now be dead, or a vegetable. How could that be unless it was for something she might know?

'*Did* you know Donna, Geoff?'

No answer. Still the faint superior smile. Did he think he had a chance of escaping? That could only make his situation worse. If he had to be hunted down he'd be virtually admitting to some kind of guilt, if he was guilty of something more than the attack on Julia.

'Geoff,' he said, 'I'll do everything I can to help you, but you've got to explain yourself. It's the only way, you know it is.'

But he smiled calmly and silently on, though shifting his gaze to Julia, up on the terrace, still carefully holding him covered. Crane wondered if he was thinking she might not be too skilled in the use of a big gun. If so, Crane had similar misgivings. It could be that she kept one in the house to scare off any possible intruder, but had perhaps never fired one in her life. Another complication.

'Geoff,' he said flatly, 'if you're not going to say anything at all to us I'll just have to subject your actions to rigorous analysis. That's one of your phrases, yes? The thing is, I've had to accept that you were in a lot of control of the investigation because no one knew more about the case than you, not even the police in the end. And you knew everything I was doing. You could have covered your own tracks because you had the inside track.'

Anderson's eyes came slowly back to Crane's. Had they become watchful behind the fixed smile?

'Let's hypothesize, say, about Ollie Stringer. Now, we were certain Adrian or one of his pals had attacked him, right, but it could just as easily have been you. You could have been lying about being out of town. You knew the day and the time I'd be meeting Ollie. You could have lured him into the hollow yourself. And the reason for that could have been that if Ollie had been able to put me on to Adrian I might have been able to eliminate him as a suspect, because he might not have done it, might he, even though it certainly began to look as if he had when Kirsty told you who and what Adrian really was. You can see how things can be shown in a different light, can't you, unless you give us the real story?'

Crane's head felt as if it were splitting with the effort of putting together this version of events, which he couldn't convince himself could be anything near the real truth. The woman looked on, mouth slightly open, bewildered. 'I'll explain later, Julia. Let's just say that the trouble with this case has always been the way it could be seen in so many different lights.'

'Well,' she said, 'all I can say is that the more I see of him the more he looks like the man I saw with Donna at the Raven, even if I was a good way off.'

'But that had to have been Hellewell. The number you gave me was checked by the police as a Leaf and Petal car.'

Anderson's smile looked to be almost taunting now. It was becoming obvious why he wouldn't speak. It was a maze of ifs and buts and had to be nearly impossible to prove anything. There was only a single, undisputed fact: he'd attacked Julia. He'd tried to attack him too but Crane left that aside. If he *had* been involved in Donna's death, two good brains, Anderson's and a lawyer's, could surely get him off a charge which could probably only be based on paper-thin circumstantial evidence. And Julia, he was certain, was too private a person to want to bring any charge of her own against him for a blow to the head.

'Are they *sure* it was a Leaf and Petal car, Frank?' Julia said. 'The one at the Raven?'

Crane sighed, the sound leg that was having to bear the bulk of his weight beginning to ache as much as the one Anderson had struck. 'They're hardly ever wrong, Julia, they have access to a computer which stores every vehicle registration number in the country with details of the owner. It was a Renault Scenic, one of the garden centre's runabouts.'

He spoke almost mechanically, his fogged brain still grappling with other details. And then something about the car's make rang a distant bell. He thought back to when he and Anderson had gone to Leaf and Petal to talk to Hellewell, the interview Anderson had taped with

Kirsty, because Kirsty had fancied and trusted him. She'd lent him a Leaf and Petal runabout one weekend to see how he liked it.

A Renault Scenic! That was the car she'd lent him. The shock was like being given another blow.

'There could be a definite answer as to who was driving the car you saw, Julia,' he said slowly. 'I'll not go into details, but Joe Hellewell's wife lent Anderson a Leaf and Petal Renault one weekend, to try out as he was thinking of buying one.'

Anderson couldn't control a sudden intake of breath. The smile had gone and Crane seemed to see in his eyes traces of that old exasperation when Crane had picked up on something he'd overlooked. Sickened, Crane wondered if those earlier bursts of exasperation could also be seen in a different light; maybe the more things Crane had dug up that he'd not thought of the more covering up he'd been forced to do. But it *couldn't* be possible. Could it?

He said, 'I need only check with Mrs Hellewell exactly when she lent him the Scenic to see if it checks out with the night you followed Donna to the Raven.' He glanced from him to her, who seemed such a worryingly vulnerable figure with her bloodstained forehead and her dishevelled clothes. 'Think carefully, Julia, did Donna ever tell you of anything she'd done that might have involved Anderson?'

'Frank, you know I couldn't bear to hear about—'

'I know,' he said, more gently, 'but search your mind. You talked a lot together and she trusted you.'

'She was … so very discreet, poor darling.' She couldn't stop her lips quivering. 'There was only the bad dream, the photography man.'

'I'm certain he can be ruled out. But you seemed to

think she was talking about *two* men. Someone who wanted her to go away with him, that she felt was almost trying to control her, stop her living her own life.'

'I'm ... sorry, I can't add anything to that. She was crying so hard, seemed so confused. I *know* it was a premonition now.'

Crane said, 'Well, Anderson, you were aiming for Fleet Street. It must have seemed a nice idea to have gone along with someone looking like Donna.'

His smile suddenly twisted into a sneer. 'A common prostitute? You can't think I'd want to go to London with a provincial slag in tow.'

It was only the second time he'd spoken and Crane was certain it had been involuntary. 'But you couldn't have known what type of woman she was when you first got to know her. Not with someone as secretive as Donna.'

'Think a talented reporter couldn't get a trollop like her together inside a week?'

'And that's what you did?'

'I'm commenting, Frank,' he said quietly, 'not admitting.'

'What are you saying?' Julia suddenly cried, looking even more distraught, the gun-barrel shaking. 'How dare you? Donna wasn't a prostitute. She was a good, kind-hearted, hard-working girl, who looked after her family. How *dare* you?'

'What planet have you been living on?' Anderson flung back.

'I'm ... sorry, Julia,' Crane said reluctantly. 'Donna really wasn't what she seemed. Like this man, she could put on a polished act. It fooled almost everyone.'

She gazed down at them in a lengthy despondent

silence. They stood as if acting out a play beneath the glare of the powerful lamps, with a crowd of hushed spectators in the darkness beyond the hard-edged pool of light. Then she said, in a voice so low it barely carried, 'Well, I don't care. I'd not have cared what she did as long as she had time for me. That's all I ever really asked of her, to be able to go on seeing her. I could never have harmed her, whatever she did. Never, ever … and how some *man*, some piece of human rubbish …' She couldn't go on.

Despite Anderson's mastery of his features, he couldn't control a wince of pain. 'She was humping around!' he suddenly shouted. 'She was humping around, for Christ's sake! Money down, knickers off, *that* was your pure precious little angel!'

'And you warned her it had to stop?' Crane said.

The blunt words checked him like a slapped face. He began to smile in his usual detached way, as if warning himself that silence was still the best policy.

'Can you guard him, Julia, while I call the police?'

'Have you not got a mobile?'

'He threw it in the fountain.'

'The … drawing room. You know the one.'

But she spoke hesitantly, eyes troubled, as if uneasy about Crane leaving the scene. Crane was certain now she had no real mastery of the gun. What if Anderson made a run for it? Would she dare open fire in case she killed him? He knew that Anderson, with his split-second reactions, would also have picked up on her lack of confidence.

Anderson suddenly spoke again. 'You weren't the only one, Julia, wanting to help her. You were standing in line. There was Fletcher wanting to get her face in the glossies, Hellewell wanting to turn her into a logo, you wanting a companion. Well, I wanted her to be someone you *could* take to London and not have everyone think she was just another five-star call girl.'

Crane watched him warily. He wasn't commenting now, he was admitting. He couldn't begin to guess what his game was, he was just certain that with this unpredictable man there had to be one.

'So you did get to know her?'

'Norfolk Gardens bar. She was waiting for friends. We got talking, hit it off. She stopped waiting for the others and I took her to one of those fancy restaurants she was rapidly getting herself accustomed to.'

'And she was just as secretive about you as all the rest?'

Once more, that almost subliminal wince of pain. 'I told her that if she went out with me there hadn't to be any other men. I said I'd take her to London, set us up in a decent flat. She couldn't wait to get to London. I said I'd fill the gaps in her education, take her to the theatre and the opera and the art galleries. I'd show her what to read so she'd know what they were talking about, the sorts of people we'd be mixing with.'

Despite his self-control, Crane heard that slight break in his voice he'd heard in the voices of all the others who'd spoken about Donna: Mahon, Fletcher, Hellewell, Julia. Had that really been his own dream for her, to turn her into a woman who was as cultured as she was beautiful, who could speak his language like Carol and the others who met up at the Glass-house?

'So it was *you*!' Julia cried. 'You she had that frightful dream about! Wanting to change her and control her and not let her be herself.' The gun swung wildly in her hands and Crane hoped to God she didn't fire it by mistake.

'It was what she *wanted*,' Anderson told her, almost patiently. 'She wanted to get away from the Willows and make a new start. She wanted me to help her broaden her mind. All she needed was guidance, encouragement. I gave her books to read to get her started. She was thrilled, grateful. You can't believe how grateful she was that I wanted to improve her mind.'

'That's odd,' Crane said, 'the only books she had in her room at home were two Jeffrey Archer thrillers—' Crane broke off. He'd suddenly made a new connection. 'Jeffrey Archer ... *Jeffrey*. That explains the other J in the diary, doesn't it, the one who wasn't Julia? She obviously thought your name was spelt with a J and not a G. And you knew the J was you, Geoff, right?'

Anderson watched him in silence. But not with irritation this time that Crane had found yet another piece in the puzzle. It seemed more a look of resignation. Perhaps he'd not been aware that the books he'd carefully selected for her had been tossed in the wheelie-bin the minute she got home.

'I couldn't bear to take an empty-headed slapper to London, Frank,' he said at last in a low voice. 'I was crazy about her. Christ, who wasn't? But when we weren't in bed I needed someone I could talk to. Someone who'd heard of Colette and Updike and knew who'd painted *Woman in the Green Bugatti*.'

'Her looks and Carol's mind,' Crane said. 'The cake and the ha'penny.'

'You bastard!' Julia's voice was a near shriek. 'That's what men are all about. You couldn't just let her be herself, could you? *That's* what love is. You never understood that, did you? It's accepting people exactly as they are.'

'What do *you* know?' he cried. 'You'd no idea what she was. You thought she was as innocent as she looked, all sick parents and Lady of the fucking Lamp.'

'It wouldn't have mattered, you evil swine, it wouldn't have *mattered*!'

The anguished echo of her words seemed to die slowly in the scented silence. Anderson turned back to Crane. It seemed as if he needed to talk now, as if unable to control the urge to give him some idea of the way things had been. But Crane was still on full alert, convinced the reporter knew a way to get himself out of this.

'Just give yourself up, Geoff.'

A ghost of the old engaging smile briefly flickered. 'For giving Julia a tap on the head? She's in one piece, would she really get the law on me and have all the hassle of being in the paper about her private life?'

It was as if he'd read Crane's mind earlier. 'I mean about what really matters,' Crane said, with a sense of genuine sadness. 'Donna's murder.'

'Hey, hey, don't go laying that at *my* door. Hellewell's the one who's away on his toes. I simply wanted Julia's diary. To make sure my name wasn't in it. I didn't want to be linked to her. I'd not killed her, but I didn't want the hassle either. It could only have brought the kind of publicity a crime reporter can do without.'

Crane was now in a state of total confusion. Could that be true? Or had it been something he'd thought out during that lengthy early silence? It was Julia who spoke first, appearing to have fought a hard-won battle for her self-control. 'You're lying about her,' she said, almost calmly. 'You were trying to *make* her do things. Manipulate her, turn her into something she simply couldn't be. She must have hated that more than anything, must have wanted to get right away from you.' She sighed. 'I knew she'd had little education. Nothing in my house remotely interested her: the books, the paintings, the ornaments, the antiques. I stopped talking about them as I could tell she was bored. She liked to gossip and giggle, she'd ask to see programmes with names like *Casualty* and *Big Brother* that I barely knew existed. I knew from the first weekend she simply wanted to be herself and I never attempted to change her. It was enough just to know her. It was enough …'

'You were wrong!' he said, almost in desperation. 'She *wanted* to be made over, you wouldn't believe how much she longed—'

'She wanted a ticket to London, Geoff,' Crane cut him off. 'She knew exactly which buttons to press to get herself there.'

His slight flush could be seen, even in the bleaching glare of the high-powered lamps. 'She wanted to be a different woman in a different milieu,' he said angrily.

'The National Gallery and the Albert Hall and Covent Garden? Is that really what she was pining for? Sure it wasn't Stringfellows and the Hard Rock Café?'

'She just needed *guidance*!' he cried.

'For a ticket to ride. She told you what you wanted to hear, like she told everyone. Think she gave a tinker's toss about your London? The only use she had for you was to get her there.'

'What can you know, you never even met her!'

'I've learnt plenty about her. I know what she'd do for money, which was just about anything. Know what I think? I think she knew she could make it as a class A model and knew Fletcher wasn't up to it. So it had to be London, where she knew she'd be properly managed. Only London's a big, scary place to a Bradford teenager and she knew all about kids from the provinces being sucked into King's Cross rat holes overnight. So she needed someone to lean on till she found her feet. Someone she could trust to find his way around and show her the way.'

'That's not *true*,' he shouted, face a deeper red. 'She wanted my career to come first and she was going to train for a decent career of her own.'

'You must have seen through that,' Julia said in a low, tremulous voice. 'There were things about her even I couldn't accept and I was blind to almost everything. She … she said she'd be my companion if we could live in London. Yes, she'd already tried it on with me, you see. But I knew that once we were there it would be men. Modelling and men. I knew it could only bring more heartache than I already had.'

Crane said, 'Julia's right. And where do you think you'd have been once she'd got the West End sussed? A woman with her looks and stamina could earn £10,000 a day as a top model. What could you earn, even on *The Sunday Times*? Sixty, seventy grand a year? That would be make-up money to Donna.'

'But it couldn't have lasted! It would only be for a few short years till her looks—'

'By which time she'd have married a multi-millionaire. We both know how carefully she looked to her future.'

'You don't get it, do you? It was *me* she wanted. She said I was the only man who'd seen her as a complete person, with a mind as well as a body.'

'Geoff, the reason other men didn't see her as a complete person was because she was a bear of very little brain. Far-sighted and cunning, yes. She could have graduated in cunning.'

'And no one *minded*, you bastard!' Julia gave a half-sob. 'It was enough just to be with her.'

'When did the knocking begin?' Crane said. 'When did she decide you were boring her senseless about your London and your future? Was it when she twigged it could be months before you could get her to London anyway, seeing as you'd not even got the promise of a job yet? How soon was it before she began telling you you could stuff the opera and the Royal Court and the two-room flat south of the river on a salary that wouldn't keep her in shoes?'

'Shut it, Crane! Just *shut* it!'

'It's what she did to Bobby Mahon, right? Wound him up rotten, so that in the end he'd lay one on her. Patsy was positive she liked the buzz of driving Bobby to the end of his tether. Drew the line at being throttled though.'

Pallor suddenly wiped away the flush. He looked past Crane with unfocused eyes. 'I did everything for that bitch. The dinners I paid for. The promises I made. I knew I could fix her up with a respectable job: PA, gofer, public relations, God knows she had the makings. I'd pay for everything till she started working. We'd be able to dine out on my talents and her looks. But she had to put the past behind her: modelling, other men, all that shit. I *had* to be the only man in her life ...' His voice trailed off and they stood silent again in the lamps' steady glare, the water of the pool as dark as oil behind them, the façade of the great old house forming a backdrop. Crane was now certain Julia's mastery of the gun had become even more unreliable with the tears that now blurred her vision.

'That's what really did it, eh, Geoff? There'd never been a woman in your entire life who'd not thought you were Mr Wonderful. And Donna had exactly the same problem, no one could resist her. You couldn't cope with anything being the slightest bit different, could you, the pair of you? You both took it for granted you were always to be the star. Neither of you was ever going to accept the other's ego, having your own way was a God-given right. It had absolutely nothing to do with love, but neither of you knew anything about that either, did you?'

'She was a scrubber!' he screamed. 'A slag! Before I took her up she was just disco fodder. I was saving her from middle-aged swingers ready to shell out a fistful of tenners for a night's arm candy. I was the best chance she was ever going to have. A life, a career, with a man who was going somewhere in journalism. Only she'd not stop *whoring*! She was very clever, oh yes, very discreet, always a little mobile tucked away in her frillies, set to vibrate, not ring, so she could go to the loo to arrange another seventy-sov jump. But she didn't fool me, not with my experience of human trash.' He suddenly gazed at Crane with wild, staring eyes, as if a totally different man now lived inside his head. 'Then one night I told her, told her straight: it had to stop.'

He was visibly shaking. Crane had always sensed the rigid self-control he concealed behind the jokes, the smiles, the easy manner. But Crane had learnt to be very wary of people with too much control. It could mean they were bottling emotion that might be distilling itself the longer it found no outlet, and if the valve ever did blow it could cause disproportionate damage. Julia looked on stunned, mouth falling open, the gun forgotten and pointing once more towards the ground.

'What happened, Geoff,' he said quietly, 'the night you went for a walk at Tanglewood to have it all out for once and for all?'

'You can't believe,' he almost whispered, and then he shouted, 'you can't *believe* the sheer filth she could come out with, someone who looked the way she did. You can't believe the viciousness! That I didn't earn shit and I'd never earn more than shit, not in newspapers. I bored her arse off and I was rubbish in bed, and she'd either find someone else to go to London with or she'd go on her own, and all I'd ever see of her then, if I ever got there myself, would be someone driving along Park Lane in a chauffeured limo, giving me the finger and shouting "Up yours!"'

The last words were like a scream of anguish. Comedy seemed to blend absurdly with tragedy, as it sometimes did, like the two masks that symbolized the theatre. They stood in yet another silence, both he and Julia sharing, Crane felt, the same sense of profound shock.

'Give yourself up, Geoff,' Crane said finally, as calmly as he could. 'They'll get you now, whatever you do. It was a crime of passion. They'll be lenient with a man of your clean record. Ten years top whack. An open prison. You'll still be young enough to make a new start.'

He looked about him, seeming almost stupefied, as if he'd emerged from a sort of fit that had briefly blanked his mind. When he spoke again it was with the old engaging smile, which Crane now found unbearable. 'Frank, you don't seriously believe I'd go inside for a trick-artist like

Donna Jackson? I shall clear off, vanish, give myself a new identity. I shall go to America or Australia. Big places to lose yourself in. Come back to London when the dust has settled.'

'You're not going to walk away, Geoff. Julia has you covered and I'm going to ring Benson.'

'The only problem with that is that Julia's gun isn't loaded. When I was trying to find a way out of her mansion I stumbled over a cloakroom where the gun lives. It was the work of seconds to knock out the shells.'

Julia's shoulders sagged, as did Crane's spirits. It had never paid to underestimate Anderson's resourcefulness, and he'd felt all along that he'd have one final trick up his sleeve or he'd surely not have confessed to Donna's killing.

'Couldn't afford to get myself shot,' he said, faintly contemptuous. 'She may only be a scatty dyke, but she might just have got lucky and hit me by mistake. Should have provided yourself with a MAC10, dear. Quite small, easily concealed, get off twelve hundred rounds a minute.'

'You'd have got the full minute's worth, you murdering swine,' she said in a raw, bitter voice.

'You'll not get away,' Crane told him. 'Your car lights are smashed.'

'I'd not thought of using it. I'm a fast runner. I'll find a car in a side street I can hotwire. You mustn't worry about that.'

'And if I follow you?'

'On that leg? You can barely walk man. And I disabled your car too, when you ran off into the undergrowth.'

He was right. Crane's leg was so swollen and painful he'd have trouble even controlling the clutch for the next two or three days. He glanced at Julia. She shrugged apathetically. 'Give yourself up, Geoff,' he said again. 'I'm begging you. I'll do everything in my power to help you. A good counsel ...'

'No chance, Frank.' There seemed to be a genuine warmth in his eyes as they rested on Crane's. 'She did enough damage to my life just by living. It was good knowing you, even though you had me running shitless half the time. Sorry about your gammy leg and all that other stuff back there. Goodbye each.'

He suddenly turned then to make his dash for freedom. Equally suddenly the gun went off, with a deafening report in the silence.

THIRTEEN

Anderson lay quite still in the film-set brilliance. Crane clutched his head with both hands. It had been his worst fear, that she might shoot at random and hit him by mistake. He didn't understand how she'd made the gun fire at all when Anderson was supposed to have knocked out the shells. Maybe he'd been bluffing, as always. He knew she'd killed him. What a mess. What a bloody *mess*.

But then Anderson began to move. Began writhing in agony. Began cursing and yelping. Crane limped painfully to his side, got down awkwardly on one knee, yelping softly himself. Blood was seeping through Anderson's trousers from a wound in his left thigh. Julia came up behind them. She picked up the thick stick Anderson had abandoned when he'd turned to run off. She held it by the tip, with a hand wrapped in a handkerchief, tossed it at the wounded man's side. 'He was attacking you with that, right? He'd have killed you if I'd not brought him down.' She smiled thinly. 'Just so we're both reading from the same script. He'll survive, unfortunately. I should have killed him. God knows, I *wanted* to kill him, but it's a simple flesh wound that'll cause no lasting damage.' She spoke with total, clipped assurance.

'But he'd fixed it, the gun.'

'He had indeed, but an experienced shot, Frank, always checks the state of the gun. I'd reloaded.'

'You could have fooled me.'

'Quite. I wanted him to go on thinking what a superior type he was and what a silly little featherhead I was.'

'I'll get the emergency services. For both of you.'

'Bring a tea towel from the kitchen and I'll make a tourniquet. I'll watch him. Doesn't seem quite the big confident Jack the Lad he thought he was now, does he?'

Anderson was rolling about in agony, still yelping, his expression a mixture of pain and irritation. Crane felt he was angrier about being unable to react with any kind of stoicism than being stopped from escaping.

Crane got himself up slowly. 'You're an incredible shot.'

'My father taught me. Taught me how to shoot cleanly. I've shot over dogs with some of the best in the land. You see, having a daughter instead of a son was the biggest disappointment of my father's life. So he liked to *pretend* I was a boy. Shooting, fishing, riding, fast cars. The stiff upper lip at all times, even when you fell off your horse … or someone clonks you over the head with a priceless piece of bronze.'

She ran a hand through her tousled, blood-matted hair and gazed despondently towards her fine old house. 'He made a jolly good job of it. I've had problems with my gender ever since.'

Benson shook his head, grimaced. 'All those statements, all those public appeals, the sheer man hours. And that arsehole, on the phone every verse end: any news, any developments, has Mahon coughed? No wonder coppers end up distrusting everything that moves.'

'What's the form?'

'Knows his rights, you bet. Won't admit to anything. But he will.'

'How's the leg?'

'Uncomplicated flesh wound; she was spot on. Pity she didn't let her finger slip and blow the sod away. Save the taxpayer another load of moolah.' Benson lit a new cigarette. 'Anyway, we can nail him for being at the Raven with her the actual night she disappeared. We've had sight of a Barclay-card docket signed by him. And one of the waitresses recognized Donna from a photo as being with him around that time. It wasn't a face you forgot. She doesn't read the *Standard* or she might have picked up on it before.'

'The sod had incredible luck, apart from anything else,' Crane said. 'Just managing to be in a Leaf and Petal vehicle Kirsty Hellewell had lent him the night Julia followed Donna and took the number of the Scenic. It seemed it *had* to be Hellewell then. And with him and Anderson having a bit of a resemblance.'

'Ollie Stringer will be our star witness,' Benson told him. 'He still can't speak, but we showed him a picture of Anderson and told him we'd got him banged up and would he identify him? He was nodding so hard fit to make his bloody head drop off. And if Ollie identifies him in court I reckon we're home and dry.' He ground out the cigarette angrily. 'Christ, the last person in the frame was always going to be the *Standard*'s sodding crime reporter!'

'His luck kicked in from day one,' said Crane. 'You lot

were certain Mahon had killed her. Me too. At the start I just felt it was my job to try and *prove* he'd killed her. Anderson's off the hook, even though he was never really on it. He knows perfectly well Mahon must have had some other reason to stick with the story he was home that night. He gets so confident Mahon will always stick to it that he can even take me to the Goose and Guinea and pretend to ruffle his feathers a bit.

'But he loathes Mahon personally, like all the men Donna had known, and makes his only real mistake. He feeds Mahon the stuff about the Willows pointing the bone. That blew the door open. Mahon confesses but you could clear him. I reckon that's got to be Anderson's worst hour. And then I get Adrian's name from Ollie and he knows that if I get through to Adrian and put you on to him it'll be Bobby Mahon all over again, in fact anyone I can turn up who just *might* have done it. He's shitting bricks by now and terrified that sooner or later I might get through to him. He knows I don't give in too easily and I bring a fresh mind. But then the luck's with him again. Kirsty tells him Joe Hellewell is also known as Adrian. And Adrian's dodgy lifestyle makes him seem so guilty as to almost rule out anyone else. So he makes Hellewell appear to leg it, which means he's virtually admitting his guilt. Anderson's home and dry. Except that now I'd turned up Julia Gregson.'

Crane drank some of his G and T. 'Julia was the wild card and this *really* spooks him. She keeps a proper diary and he's terrified his name might crop up in it, in the parts she'd not wanted me to read.'

'And it's him who breaks into Patsy's?'

'He's got a good fix on the way my mind works now

and he gambles on me spotting the flip chart's been tampered with. He's certain I'll decide it must have been Hellewell. Hellewell reads the chart, realizes he's the chief suspect, and he too believes he has to get his hands on that diary. So he tries to steal it, only Julia surprises him, and in the struggle he accidentally kills her. He has to leg it for good then, because if he's not nailed for one killing he'll be nailed for another. That's what we're *meant* to think when Julia's body's found. What Anderson didn't bargain for was me picking up on how crucial the diary could be *before* he'd managed to see off Julia. Well, you can't think of everything, not even Anderson, who can have few equals for tying up loose ends. I was certain Julia might be in danger, and she was, but not from Hellewell.'

Benson lit another cigarette, inhaled deeply. 'What we can't figure is why Hellewell went off with Anderson the night he disappeared. We've enhanced the CCTV footage. Still can't get the number but know it's definitely a Honda Accord.'

'I've not stopped kicking it around. We know why Anderson and Donna ended up at Tanglewood that night. He'd bought her a fancy meal, she'd be staying the night at his flat probably, but he wanted a neutral place in between where he could read her the riot act about sleeping around. Well, that's where he lost it, throttled the poor kid and bunged her in the reservoir, where she'd be now if it hadn't been for the youngster finding her. Well, I'm certain it was a crime of passion, but quick thinker that he is he knew how to make sure the body was weighted before he dumped it. But it must have struck him later that reservoirs make handy burial grounds. I began to wonder if maybe he took Hellewell to the next reservoir along the line. That would be Scamworth. It's very, very quiet and too far out for kids to get there on foot and use as a swimming pool.'

Benson's mouth went down sceptically at the corners. 'Can't see it myself. Hellewell was a tough bloke, like Anderson. How's he going to let himself be lured from Leaf and Petal?'

'Lure's a good word. It took me a while to get there, but we have to remember that Hellewell was a fiver each way, and that Anderson's tall and good looking with a well made body. What if he told Hellewell he'd always fancied him, couldn't get him off his mind, how did he feel about going somewhere quiet and doing something about it? Like a beauty spot with a reservoir attached? That's only a theory, I'm trying to think like Anderson might have done.'

'I'll bear it in mind,' Benson said grudgingly. Crane knew he would and if the theory was acted on Benson would quietly claim it as his own, touchy as he was about Crane's superior deductive skills, about his way of obsessively worrying at a problem till something gave. He knew Benson often felt exposed since he'd left the force, though would never admit it. It was very sad. They'd been a good team together, apart from their close friendship, as Benson had solid police skills of his own. It was just that a few things had gone adrift in Benson's mind this past two or three years.

'You're right about his luck though,' Benson said dourly.

'Even with his car. I never even knew he *drove* a Honda. For one reason or another he was in a pool car or in my car or parked out of sight. And he made his own luck with the flip chart. The sod simply sets it up, says it'll keep us all in the picture. Keep *him* in the picture! It just meant he never lost track of what I was up to, not for a minute, because I was writing it all down even when he wasn't there. It was a game he couldn't lose.'

Benson shook his head. 'Why did he go on like that? Pretending he'd never give in on the case till someone put their hand up?'

'I think he saw it as a good way of drawing the fire well away from himself. Like those blokes who go on the telly now and then, tears in their eyes, appealing for information about a wife or a partner who's bought it. And then it turns out that the guy who's doing the appealing did the business.

'I also think, in some part of his mind, once she was dead, he knew it was just about the best story he'd ever had. Apart from all the reports and articles he could write about it he was planning this big feature about the innocent victim he was going to make her out to be of a Willows going to the dogs. He was aiming to syndicate it and use it as a crucial part of his CV when he made his bid for a London job.'

'Why did he write her up as such an innocent? He could maybe have shown the Willows in a worse light still if he'd said it had turned her into a tom.'

'I don't honestly think he could ever stop seeing her the way she was when he first got to know her, when she *seemed* innocent. A bit of a chatterbox, a bit empty-headed, but that was because of the Willows and poor schooling. And he could take her away from all that, make her over into a fit companion for a college man. Like Svengali, he'd soon have her singing in tune. But he twigged very quickly about the whoring and the dodgy men and the vicious tongue, and yet in his mind I think he always wanted her to be the sweet little kid he'd seen in the clubs with the strobes flashing on her hair.'

'He always seemed such a decent bloke. Everyone liked him at the nick. Especially the women.'

'That was his trouble, the women had been there for him all his life. It wasn't just his looks, he was clever, funny, bags of charm. And then the only woman he can't get off his mind can take him or leave him. He might be good looking but he's never going to be a millionaire, and funny and clever were never going to replace money in Donna's mind. The very worst thing he could have done was to think he could educate her. He knew the glamour just wasn't going to be enough. But all *she* wanted was a London address. He could stick the culture. I bet inside a fortnight she'd have been wondering if it was worth the hassle. She had a short fuse and she was masterclass at sticking the knife where it would do the most damage, and danger excited her. I reckon Anderson couldn't believe it was happening to him, some chit of a girl telling him he had a crap future and wasn't up to much under the duvet.'

'All right,' Benson growled, 'he got carried away. It happens. Christ, we know if anyone does. But how did this clean cut college boy go on living with himself?'

'The way most killers do these days, now that guilt and blame and remorse are out of fashion. I don't think he regarded himself as being all that guilty, or that his future was worth ruining for a call girl. I think he'd virtually convinced himself that with the men she ran around with, and that mouth of hers, she was going to get herself topped one day anyway; it was his bad luck he happened to be first in line. And then, writing about her so much I think it almost objectified her in his mind. I think she'd begun to transmute into the sweet innocent kid who'd been murdered, and the killer could have been anyone. Anyone but him, anyway.'

'What about Ollie and Joe Hellewell? He's going to objectify them too, is he?'

'Give him time. Maybe it gets easier after you've done it once.'

'Well, he's going to have plenty of time to mull it all over, that's for sure.'

'The sad thing, the really sad thing is that he'd convinced himself he'd be rescuing Donna from her background. He could make her happy, give her a decent life. But she wasn't *unhappy*. She was having a ball. She *liked* screwing around and making a few bob. And she had her life mapped out for when she got to London. She'd sleep with some big name photographer and she'd be up and running as a model all the magazines wanted. Inside six months she'd have nailed a stock exchange trader. She was a total realist. I reckon dream girls usually are. It was the blokes who were doing the real dreaming about those dazzling futures they had in mind for her. *She* was making meticulous plans for a future that would be exactly right for the type of woman she was. And why not, poor bitch?'

Benson nodded, finished his drink, got up to go. 'Well, I'll be off. We'll keep you in the picture. See you.' He'd begun to walk away, when he slowly turned back. 'Well done, Frank, it's saved us a hell of a lot of extra work.'

Crane nodded, knowing the effort it had cost him to say

those words, after the months of effort he and the others had put in on the case, which Crane appeared to have sorted out in a couple of weeks. But Crane knew he'd had luck apart from skill. And he couldn't forget that harmless old Ollie had been dreadfully injured, and Hellewell almost certainly disposed of, before he could deliver a killer to the police. As anything to do with murder nearly always was, it had been a Phyrric victory.

They sat motionless in their tiny cluttered living room. Malc's hand shook on his glass of whisky, and tears slid once again down Connie's face.

'He spent the whole evening with us,' Malc said, in a low raw voice. 'Making notes for what he'd put in the paper. About her life and when she was growing up. He couldn't have been more sympathetic. Mam and me, we couldn't stop filling up, and he'd comfort us. He'd *comfort* us, Frank! And it was *him*. Dear God ...'

'It couldn't have come as a bigger shock, Malc,' Crane told him.

'And then, when I heard you were working together, I said, "We've got two grand lads on the case, Mam, two grand lads." Weren't those my very words, Mam?'

'And he'd been going out with her,' Connie said, in a voice little more than a whisper. 'A nice, well spoken boy like that from a good home. I can't weigh it up, Frank, I can't weigh it up at all.'

'If he'd just *confessed*!' Malc cried. 'It wouldn't have made it no better, but to carry on as if it weren't nothing to do with him.'

'He'll go inside for a very long time, Malc. He's going to plead not guilty and that'll mean a long expensive trial.

The judge won't overlook it when it comes to sentencing him.'

'Well ... we know the truth now,' Connie said, dabbing her eyes. 'We can't thank you enough. You put yourself in such a lot of danger. He could have killed you too.'

'We couldn't bear not knowing, Frank. You've done wonders,' Malc said, his own eyes now wet with tears. He reached out blindly to grasp his daughter's hand. 'And we've got our Patsy. I don't know how we'd have got on without our Patsy, bless her.'

Patsy reddened slightly. Crane felt that at least some kind of closure was in sight. They'd never forget their golden girl, but she could finally be laid to rest. Maybe now it would be Patsy's turn to receive some of the love and attention she'd always anyway deserved so much more than her calculating, beautiful tramp of a sister.

'How much do we owe you, Frank?' Connie said in a more collected tone. 'We got the insurance cheque through the other day.'

'Don't you worry about that now, Connie,' he said gently. 'My lady at the office will sort it out presently.' He got up. 'Need a lift, Patsy?'

'I'll stay with Mam and Dad tonight, Frank.'

He kissed Connie's pale cheek, took Malc's trembling hand in both his own. At the door, Patsy said, 'I'll be back at the flat tomorrow night. Will you come for a drink?'

The others sat together, but she sat in a corner, alone. The Glass-house seemed to have a subdued atmosphere without Anderson laughing and joking from the chair that had always been reserved for him at the head of one of the central communal tables, not very long ago.

He sat down with her. She gave him a pale-featured smile. The contrast couldn't have been sharper with the rosy cheeks and the impish grins he'd known before. 'Thanks for coming, Frank.'

'My pleasure, Carol. Drink?'

'No thanks, this one will do me.' She passed a hand through her curly black hair, her green eyes meeting his with a clouded look.

'I'm very, very sorry about Geoff, Carol.'

She nodded, giving an impression of fatigue, as if she'd not slept much recently. 'I need your advice, Frank.'

'Go ahead.'

'It wasn't Geoff. You must know that as well as I do. This is madness! You have police contacts, haven't you? I need to speak to someone. It's very urgent.'

He watched her in silence for a few seconds. 'I only wish it wasn't Geoff. I liked him. That's the problem when someone you like does something dreadful. But the evidence—'

'But it's all circumstantial! Every bit of it.'

'Maybe about Donna's actual killing, yes, but when all the other things come out in court.'

'Where was he supposed to be the night she disappeared?'

'These are police matters now, Carol. I can't say too much as I'll be a prosecution witness. You know how it is.'

'He was at the Raven, wasn't he? I bet they're making out he was with her. Well, he wasn't! He was with me!'

He sighed, gave her a wry glance. 'The waitress identified—'

'It was me, Frank. I wrote it in my last year's diary.'

'When? Last night?'

'Don't be such a shit.'

'Look, Carol, I don't want to upset you more than you already are, but you must have known he was seeing someone else around the time she died. Women always know. And you know he's never been the same with you since. And that's because he's never got her off his mind.' He put a hand on hers. 'I know what you're going through. And it won't be any consolation, but you were exactly right for him: in the business, well educated, outgoing. And you've always been there for him, hoping he'd be back one day as the Geoff you used to know. Well, you're going to need that level head of yours, and the way you feel about him, because in the end he's going to need you like he's never needed anyone in his life. If you're prepared to wait.'

Her cheeks were suddenly flushed, her eyes blazing with anger. 'Don't patronize me, Frank. Just tell me who I need to speak to at the station. Just give me a name.'

'It won't get you anywhere. They'll accuse you of wasting police time and they'll get very angry. Girlfriends are always trying this on, Carol, believe me.'

'Just give me a name.'

'Benson. DS Ted Benson. And don't mention my name.'

'You could help me if you wanted to. You know it's not Geoff. *Geoff*? He'd give you the shirt off his back. His father's a professor, a *professor*, for Christ's sake. His mother's a doctor and a JP. He couldn't have done it.'

He sighed again. Connie Jackson had already pointed out his impeccable middle-class credentials. 'It doesn't always follow, Carol, you know it doesn't. You should do, you're a journalist.'

'If it wasn't for you the poor sod wouldn't be on remand,' she cried bitterly. 'I wish to Christ he'd never set eyes on you.'

'I can understand that, but let's not forget there's an eighteen-year-old girl involved here, who had her entire life in front of her. And if he's guilty, and proved to be guilty, he'll have to serve his sentence.'

'He ... is ... not ... guilty,' she said, spacing the words with trembling lips. 'And if some arsehole of a counsel tries to ... to manipulate everything so it *seems* he is I'll never stop searching for the truth. I'll hire a proper investigator and I'll never give in, never, never, never ...'

She burst into tears. There was nothing he could do to calm her, as she wouldn't listen or let him touch her. She was still weeping when he got up to go, her friends anxiously crossing from their table to hers.

He was middle-sized, slender and dark haired, with brown eyes. He had a warm and easy smile. 'How do you do, Mr Briggs.' Crane shook his hand. 'Sit down and tell me how I might be able to help you.'

'I'll not waste your time,' he said. 'Mind if I call you Frank? I'm Henry.'

'Go ahead, Henry.'

'It's about a girl called Donna, a reporter, a dodgy photographer, a wealthy lesbian, an abusive boyfriend and a man who owns a garden centre, whose body police divers are searching for in Scamworth reservoir even as we speak. And the reporter is in the frame.'

'You another journalist? How do you know all this?'

His smile had the breezy look he'd so often seen in Anderson. 'Come on, Frank, an old China hand like you wouldn't expect a London investigative reporter to reveal any sources, would you?'

'It would depend on what you wanted from me.'

'Frank, there's a powerful scent coming out of Bradford. It's the scent of one of the best crime stories of the decade. It's got the lot: a dead beauty, a crime the police can't solve, a man who puts his hand up when he's not guilty, a PI who teams up with the reporter to find the real killer, and a reporter who works the clock round on a murder he committed himself.'

'He's not stood in the dock yet.'

'Agreed, but the feeling is, with that lot stacked against him, he'd better start getting used to prison food.'

He'd got it all right, but Crane was saying nothing to any reporters that might one day prejudice the case. He smiled. 'No comment.'

'Frank, this is nothing to do with routine reporting. All the papers are circling for that particular kill. I'm talking the paperback here, that's going to be rushed out the minute the verdict's in place. You know, that'll be in every supermarket and petrol station, every airport and chain store. But it's no deal unless I can get your input.'

'I'm sorry to disappoint you.'

'There's an advance involved,' he said. 'I'll split it with you and give you a small percentage of the royalties. That gives you two and a half grand in your back pocket. All you do is talk to me. I do the rest; writing, promoting, publicity.'

'I'm sorry,' Crane said firmly. 'It's tempting, but if there's one thing I price above rubies it's my anonymity. It would get the punters twitchy. They might think I'm getting too big to chase a debt for them or a husband who's running loose.'

'No one's going to know about our private deal. And I'll write it as if I've dug out most of the detail on my own, while paying due tribute to you for "the valuable help you gave me."' He put fingers up to indicate quotation marks for the last words.

Crane hesitated. He could find a good use for the money.

'It might even run to a film or a teleplay. You'd be down for a piece of that too.'

'The trouble is, Henry, I've got to know Donna's parents very well. They're two really decent types and they worshipped the kid. If this book had a big success they'd have to live through losing her all over again, when they're just beginning to get their heads right.'

'I understand that. I've got a kid sister of my own. But the thing is, it won't just be me thinking there's a book in this. Some very mangled versions could find their way into the pipeline. If you and me were to cooperate it'll be the exact truth, sympathetically told. Once the rest know I'm getting it from the horse's mouth they'll back off.'

Crane watched him. He couldn't argue with that. Whatever he did he was never going to be able to protect them from having to keep reliving Donna's short life and appalling death.

'All right,' he said cautiously. 'I'd need approval of the final draft. I mean that and I'd want it in writing.'

'Agreed. I'm currently on leave and staying at the Norfolk. I'll be spending the time getting a feel for the area: the Willows, the SOC, the clubs and so on. If we could spend a couple of evenings talking it through on tape, that's all I'd need. Anything else, I can ring you.'

'I can make it tomorrow evening and probably the one after.'

'Great. We can have a meal sent up to my room.' He held out his hand. 'Thanks, Frank, I'll give it my best shot.'

Crane held open the door of his little office for him. 'Tell me,' he said, 'if you were absolutely obsessed with a beautiful hooker and she made you so angry you topped her and then managed to cover your tracks, would you have so much printer's ink in your veins you could then try to turn it into the biggest story of your career?'

He smiled the engaging smile again that was so reminiscent of Anderson's. He didn't nod. But he didn't shake his head either.

That evening, as his car was idling at traffic lights, Crane saw a billboard outside a newsagent's. It said: BODY FOUND IN SCAMWORTH RESERVOIR.

There were fresh flowers in the tiny flat and the window stood open on the warm still evening. He said, 'We could go for a meal. We never did have a chance to celebrate your promotion.'

'We could … eat in, if you like,' she said hesitantly. 'I've brought some things from work I can put in the oven.'

'Fine by me.' He sipped a little of the gin and tonic she'd made him.

'I could do with a quiet evening.'

'Hard day?'

She nodded, smiled. 'Robert's looking after me. He's the manager in charge of my section. He's nice. Keeps us at it, but he works very hard too.'

'Good. I hope you're giving the impression you've got your eye on his job when he gets his next promotion.'

'Oh, Frank …'

She wore a lemon cotton shirt over skinny black pants,

and her smooth hair gleamed in declining sunlight. He thought again of the woman she'd been on that first evening: fright hair, wrinkled clothes, sunk in an apathy she'd not bothered to conceal. He knew she was now a woman who was going somewhere. She was beginning to get on and she liked it, liked it a lot. He could see her in ten years, a valued senior employee, her plain looks enhanced by maturity. He wondered again if he really had been responsible for any of that. He'd given her a word or two of encouragement, involved her in that tortuous search for her sister's killer, but the rest had been all her own doing.

'I'm not going to charge your folks for the work I've done, Patsy. They can't afford it and apart from that I've had an unexpected windfall.'

'You can forget that,' she said briskly. 'I know you're trying to be kind, but there's no way they'll let you work for nothing.'

'Right, I'll send them a bill and when they pay I'll give you the money. Add that to the money of Donna's the police will be returning to you and give the lot to your mum and dad to help with the deposit for the bungalow. Say you've touched a win on the Lottery.'

'No, Frank, you're not a charity.'

'I agree. I'm not normally in the habit of letting anyone off a penny, whatever their station. But your people are different. They've suffered too much and they deserve a break. And I can assure you it'll not leave me out of pocket.'

'Well, if you insist,' she said reluctantly.

They sat over their drinks as a darker blue filtered across a clear sky. 'Is Chinese all right with you?' she said.

'That'll do fine.'

'Will … Sancerre go with it? Is that how you pronounce it?'

'Sancerre. That's posh. I didn't know you were into wine.'

She grinned. 'You know bloody well I'm not. I went to the wine department and told Ivan I wanted a nice wine for someone I knew would appreciate it.'

'That was very thoughtful.'

They sat for a while in silence. 'Thank you for helping me,' she said then quietly. 'Believing in me.'

It was as if she'd read his mind. 'Patsy, it was all there, the urge to make something of your life. All I did was encourage you.'

'It's so funny … what people can do to you. I feel like a different woman because I got to know you. You're just the same but I'm so different.'

'Well, I'm very glad if you think I've been able to help.'

'I can't begin to thank you.'

'The Chinese is thanks enough. Not forgetting the Sancerre.'

'It'll be ready soon. Could … we have a proper night out though? At the weekend maybe?'

'I'll be away, I'm afraid. A friend who lives in Gargrave.'

'A … a girlfriend?'

They were sitting on the little sofa. He took her hand. 'I see her once or twice a month. The rest of the time we live our own lives. She lost the man she was going to marry in very tragic circumstances, and me … well, I lost the woman I loved because she met someone she liked better. But the relationship I have with Colette suits us both.'

He wished he'd not had to say any of that, but it had to

be said sooner or later. He knew he'd make her very unhappy. The animation had already faded in her lavender eyes, the smile left lips which now trembled slightly. He'd known it was going to be difficult as he still felt the pain of his own old wounds, the night Vicky had told him how much she liked him, liked him more than most men she'd known, including the new one, and she was sorry but she didn't love him. And that's how it was with him and Patsy. It wasn't her plain looks; he lived with plain looks himself. And he liked her, liked her an awful lot, but no more.

'I suppose she's very glamorous and pretty?' she said, in a small sad voice.

Crane sighed. Poor kid, it always came back to her looks in her own mind. A single tear ran down the side of her nose. 'Hey, hey,' he said gently, '*I'd* be no good for you. I work twelve hour days, six, seven days a week. I've got so much baggage I'd need a truck. What you need is a nice bloke like Robert.'

She gave him a sidelong glance. 'How do you know? How do *you* know he fancies me?'

'The way you sounded when you told me about him. I bet he'd like to take you out, wouldn't he?'

'Is that what makes you such a good PI,' she said, her voice still wavering. 'Because you can tell things from how people speak?'

'Look, Patsy, if he's a decent type, think about it. You want kids, don't you, one day, like most women? A nice home and lifestyle?'

'His mother died recently,' she almost whispered. 'He looked after her. They say that's why he didn't go steady with anyone, so he could look after his mam. They say he's the salt of the earth. They say a woman couldn't go wrong who took up with Robert, the way he looked after his mam.'

Tears she couldn't control began to brim along her lids. Crane continued holding her hand, wishing he could spare her some of the unhappiness. Yet he had a feeling that in all the excitement of getting her promotion, of feeling she had a future, of buying new clothes, she was possibly confusing gratitude with genuine attraction. He was certain she'd be over him one day, would begin to see a life more suited to her with a man like Robert, who'd be able to give her so many of the things it was beyond Crane to provide.

He wondered if he should have kept his distance, despite her crucial value to the case. Been non-committal, let her work out her own salvation, let her know from the start he was off limits. If he were honest with himself, he knew there'd always been a suspect pleasure in believing he was encouraging her to make herself over, helping her to tease out the comely and ambitious woman she was now on her way to becoming. But the end result just seemed to be Patsy weeping with a different kind of unhappiness.

He sighed. At least his involvement had been totally benign. All he'd done was point her towards things she'd always wanted for herself anyway. That had been Anderson's biggest mistake. He'd wanted to remould Donna into something she'd simply not wanted to be. He'd had his own dream for her just like all the others, but unlike them he'd tried to impose it. He'd never grasped what damage dreams could do, especially the impossible ones. And in trying to impose that dream he'd overlooked

Karl Popper's law, that he himself had once quoted: the law of unintended consequences. In his case, the dream girl herself ending her short gaudy life at the bottom of Tanglewood reservoir.